LITTLE BIRD

ADVANTAGE PLAY SERIES-BOOK THREE

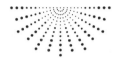

KELSIE RAE

Cover Art by Sly Fox Cover Designs
Editing by My Brother's Editor
Proofreading by Stephanie Taylor
February 2020 Edition
Published in the United States of America

CHAPTER ONE

LITTLE BIRD

Two weeks earlier

I don't know how I got here. Not really. I remember walking down the street before a strange set of arms wrapped around my waist, and the burning prick of a needle pressed into my neck. After that? Darkness.

That is until I woke up in an office surrounded by naked women who were just as beaten—just as bloodied —as me. When I saw Burlone behind the desk, my pulse spiked, and my breathing grew shallow before I remembered the importance of not letting them *see*. I can't let them see the real me or my real emotions. No. I need to be numb.

Fifteen minutes later, I was dragged into an empty room with a twin-sized bed in the center of it. Then I was left alone in nothing but a black bra and matching bikini cut underwear, which is where I find myself now. Looking around the space, I notice a pair of handcuffs attached to the metal bed frame and struggle to pull my eyes away from the promise they hold.

I never thought I'd find myself here. Although, now that I think about it, I'm not sure anyone really does. Still, my entire life has been spent in a different kind of prison to keep me from a fate like this. My eyes fill with tears when I realize they were right. My father. My brother. Everyone. A girl like me will never be safe. She'll never be normal. She'll never be anything at all.

Inhaling a shaky breath, I hold it for ten seconds then release it through my mouth. But on the next inhale, the lingering scent of pee that clings to the stained mattress burns my nostrils, making me cough.

I'm in so much freaking trouble.

Panicking, I force my eyes closed and squeeze them shut as tight as I possibly can.

I'm screwed. I'm so screwed. I'm so freaking screwed.

The mantra continues over and over again before I drive my fingernails into the palm of my hand in hopes that the bite of pain will ground me. With another deep breath, I dig deep and search for the courage to look around the rest of the room. Opening my eyes, I do another quick scan of my prison. Other than the bed and a medium-sized Home Depot bucket tucked in the corner, it's empty. The walls are made of cinder blocks, the floors are nothing but a slab of cement, and there aren't any windows. As soon as I come to that realization, I feel the walls pressing in from all sides.

I think I'm going to be sick.

CHAPTER TWO

DEX

"*H*ey, man. Burlone wants to see you in his office," Sei greets me with a shit-eating grin as I step inside the lobby of Sin.

"Why? I've already clocked out. I need some sleep."

"Don't be a pussy, Dex. It's not like your job last night was that rough." He's talking about my orders to kick the shit out of an innocent girl for beating my boss in a game of poker. My hands close into tight fists, and the bruised knuckles burn at the memory. I've never hit a girl before earlier tonight. And I'm pretty sure I've never felt lower than when I landed that first punch, either. Pinching the bridge of my nose, I release a sigh then drop my head back to look toward the blood-colored ceiling of the Allegretti-owned casino, Sin.

I took my time coming back here after I left the girl passed out on her apartment floor with a swollen face and a cold reminder that no one messes with the Allegretti family. No one. And especially not a girl who publicly humiliated the boss on national television before skipping off into the distance with a cashier's check in her back pocket that Burlone Allegretti had never planned on losing.

My gaze shoots down to my front pocket, where the flimsy piece of paper is neatly folded for safekeeping. I shouldn't have come back here. I should've kept walking around the empty streets, wondering how different my life could've been if my father had accepted me as his own. But as the sun began to creep up over the horizon, I found myself in front of Sin with the expectation of collapsing onto my bed and sleeping for a solid ten hours. Unfortunately for me, Sei got to me first.

"I said I'm done for the night," I grit out in hopes of escaping to my room.

Reaching out, an amused Sei grabs my bicep, stopping me in my tracks. "Do whatever the hell you want, but don't say I didn't relay the message." A cigarette in hand, Sei places it between his lips before letting go of me as his other hand searches for a lighter in his pocket.

"Later, Sei," I mumble, turning toward the elevators.

He doesn't bother to answer.

Hustling through the lobby of the casino, I adjust my suit and press the 'up' button. When it arrives, I hover my finger over the floor that will lead me to my suite on the top floor.

"Shit," I curse under my breath before hitting the one that leads to Burlone, instead.

I'm not in the mood for this.

With a knock on the office door, I wait for Burlone's invitation.

"Get the fuck in here."

Twisting the handle, I step inside.

"Sei said you wanted to see me?"

"Yeah. Take a seat."

I grab the closest chair I can find and sit my ass down then wait for him to get to the point. Crossing my arms over my chest, I lean back and hold his stare.

"You're awfully pissy this morning."

"Long night," I grunt.

His lips tilt up in amusement before he rests his elbows on the table and steeples his fingers, brushing his index fingers against the dimple on his chin. "Aw, yes. Sometimes I forget how much you hate hitting women. Interesting that you don't mind working for me. Ironically, that's why I called you in here."

With a slow swallow, I probe, "And why's that? No offense, Burlone, but like I've said, I had a long night and want to go to bed. Is that a problem?"

I know I'm pushing my luck by the way his amusement vanishes and is replaced with barely contained frustration. "Wanna try that again, Dex? Maybe with a little more respect this time?"

Respect? I almost laugh at the ridiculousness of it. I've never respected the guy, but I do respect the power he wields.

My jaw is clenched as I search for the self-preservation to give a shit. It takes me a few seconds to find it. Releasing a sigh, I try again. "You're right, Boss. I'm sorry I'm being short. I haven't slept in almost"—I lift my wrist to check the time on my watch—"thirty-two hours, and I'm a little tired. Won't happen again."

Burlone's nod of approval sets me at ease. "Good. Since you're tired, I'll get straight to the point. I have a new job for you. One that will likely not involve punching anything for the next two weeks, so you should consider it a vacation. All you have to do is keep an eye on some fruit. That's it."

Fruit is a slang term we use for the women he's selling. The women his men have collected who are kept in tiny rooms in the basement while Burlone either sets up a buyer or uses them for their bodies like a punching bag with holes. On occasion, he's asked someone to watch over a particularly valued piece of fruit until he can get her transported. His men have no self-discipline and have never been good at following orders, so it's always a risk to leave them alone with the fruit for long periods of time. However, I've always kept a wide berth from the human trafficking aspect, and I don't like the feeling of being dragged in with Burlone's request.

"That's never been my job before," I grit out.

He waves me off. "Yes, well, I've never had such a variety of fruit before and don't want it to spoil before the tournament."

My brows pinch, my head tilting in confusion before asking, "What tournament?"

I barely survived this one.

With a wicked grin, a satisfied Burlone sits back in his chair and explains, "You've been with me for a long time, Dex. But I think you were a kid when I started hosting these tournaments. Ones where we gamble with things other than money. And in two weeks, I've decided to hold another one."

"Which is why you need me to make sure the fruit doesn't spoil before then." I shake my head as my blood starts to boil. "You and I had an agreement, Boss. I'd be your muscle. I'd kick the shit out of anyone you asked me to without asking questions. I'd collect any debt that was owed to you. Those were my requirements when I requested and accepted the job."

He scoffs. "You were ten when I found you on the streets, Dex. Hell, I practically raised you, and you were begging to work for me by the time you turned sixteen. Don't pretend you're a martyr. Don't act like you shouldn't be worshipping me like a god for saving you. I understand you're a little skittish because of your whore of a mother and the things you saw as a kid, but I think it's about time you grow the hell up. I need you to take care of a few girls. Make sure they're fed. Make sure my men keep their hands to themselves. And make sure they're where they need to be when I need them to be there. That's it. Understand?"

Everything inside of me is begging to reach for the gun tucked into the waist of my slacks and pull the trigger. But I don't.

Taking a deep breath, I dig my fingers into the armrests on my chair and ask, "That's it?"

He narrows his eyes. "Yeah. That's it. Now, get the hell out of my office."

CHAPTER THREE

LITTLE BIRD

*H*uddled in the corner, I've been dozing in and out of consciousness for the past few hours when a soft knock breaks the eerie silence encompassing the room.

I don't make a sound. I don't move a muscle. And I pray to any gods who might be listening that I can somehow find a way to melt into the rough cinder blocks behind me, letting me disappear.

The jingling of keys makes me cower further, burrowing into the corner until the skin along my back is raw.

With a squeak, the door opens slowly, cautiously, before a man appears through the gap. My mouth opens in shock when I think I recognize him before he steps out of the shadow, and I see his face more fully. *It's not him.* The man in front of me looks like he's in his late twenties––maybe early thirties if the years were rough on him. His hair is cropped short, and a white button-up shirt covers his massive biceps and chest. My terror spikes with the knowledge this man could crush me like an ant.

I watch as he scans the bed, his brows furrowing in confusion before searching the rest of the room and landing on my tiny frame huddled in the corner.

"Hey." His tone is soft as he raises his hands in the air in an attempt to look harmless. Slowly, he takes a step forward, trying not to scare me.

It doesn't work.

Pulling my arms across my almost-naked chest while hoping to cover the important bits that are currently on display, I scramble farther into the corner.

"Shh...," he shushes, his feet stopping his pursuit. "I'm not going to hurt you."

A dry laugh escapes me, but it comes out more like a squeak.

"I promise," he continues, "I'm not going to hurt you. I'm here to take care of you and make sure no one touches you. Understand?"

Taking him in, he looks so sincere. If it were any other situation, I might believe him. But I'm not stupid. I've been kidnapped, am being held against my will, and am locked in a room with nothing but a dirty mattress that smells like pee and a few pairs of handcuffs. I mean, come on.

As he looks closer, his jaw clenches before his fingers start unbuttoning his shirt, disproving his comment from only thirty seconds ago.

I don't bother begging him not to touch me. It'd only be a waste of breath. Instead, I just hold his stare as he slides the shirt from his muscular torso until he's in nothing but a pair of slacks and a white undershirt. When the crisp fabric hits my face, I tug it away, then look up at him with confusion.

He surprises me by squatting down, then sitting on the cold cement a few feet away to give me plenty of space. I find myself frozen, unable to move a muscle.

"Put it on." He lifts his chin to the shirt I'm clutching in my hands.

Again, I don't move.

"This isn't a trick," he mutters. "I'll even close my eyes if you want me to. It's cold as hell in here, and I doubt you like being naked and vulnerable."

Chewing on the inside of my cheek, I slowly unfold my body with the shirt still acting as a barrier between us. When we both realize I'm going to have to reveal my nearly bare body to him in order to wrap the shirt around me, he closes his eyes. "Five seconds. Don't try anything stupid."

Quickly, I slide my arms into the sleeves then attempt to button the front within the allotted time of privacy, but my fingers are numb from the cold, and I struggle to push each little button through the loop. Finally, my fumbling attempt is successful, and I look up to find him watching me.

"Time's up," he mutters.

I swallow, refusing to take in all the glorious olive skin within arm's reach. This is probably some ploy to get into my pants without me fighting him. *Show her a bit of kindness, and she'll spread her legs with ease.* I grit my teeth and bring my eyes back to his.

"I'm Dex," he introduces himself.

The awkward silence is suffocating, but I don't know what to say.

"What's your name?" he probes.

With glassy eyes, I blink. "Are you serious right now?"

A puzzled expression is all I get in reply, forcing me to continue, "Were you not there for Burlone's little speech? How he stripped us of our clothes then stripped us of our names, telling us we're nothing but helpless little pieces of fruit, ripe for the picking." I release a shaky breath.

"You're not a piece of fruit."

I scoff, wiping away a stray tear as it rolls down my cheek.

"You aren't," he insists. "If anything, I'd say you're a little bird who was placed in a cage and is begging to be set free."

"Then I guess that's what you should call me. Little Bird. Because I don't think I'll ever be the same person I once was."

With a nod, he stands to his full height, towering over me. "I think we finally found something we can both agree on, Little Bird."

I don't bother to look up at him. Instead, I stay focused on his loafers and dark slacks as he retreats to the door, closing it behind him.

CHAPTER FOUR

DEX

"So, how's the fruit holding up?" Sei asks with a wicked grin. He's lazily sitting back in his chair with another damn cigarette hanging from the side of his mouth.

Images of each of them flash through my mind before stopping on Little Bird huddled in the corner. With a subtle shake of my head, I scatter the memories and reply, "As good as can be expected. Some of them are a little bruised, though. Aren't you supposed to be a bit more careful with the merchandise?" I can't help the bite that accompanies my question, followed by a dull headache in the back of my skull.

I need a fucking vacation.

"Meh." He shrugs, seeming amused, yet indifferent. "We got a lot of exotic fruit this time around, though; am I right? I mean, did you get a look at the passion fruit?" With his fingers pressed to his lips, he kisses them dramatically like a good ol' Italian appreciating a fine wine.

Passion fruit is a code word for attractive, and he's not wrong. There were multiple girls in Sei's last run that were gorgeous, including my Little Bird.

"Yeah. I've seen the passion fruit," I grumble. "The problem is keeping those types of fruit ripe and unspoiled when every one of our guys is banging on their doors for a taste. You wouldn't know anything about that, would you?"

Cutting his gaze to mine, he lets out a slow puff of smoke from his lungs, and I hold his stare with ease.

"I've been given one job, Sei. And it's to keep the fruit in good condition until they're transported. Stop sending your men to fuck with them."

"Fuck them, Dex," he corrects me with a grin. "I'm not sending them to fuck *with* them. I'm sending them to fuck them in general."

"And I'm telling you it's a bad idea. Burlone wants to make sure they're not all spoiled within a week—"

"Fuck you, Dex. I can do whatever the hell I—"

"Gentlemen, gentlemen, gentlemen," Burlone admonishes us from the hall. I hear his footsteps echo around the office as he steps across the threshold and walks to his chair behind his desk. "Is there a problem here?"

With gritted teeth, I tear my gaze from Sei and turn to Burlone. "You gave me one job, Burlone. One job. Sei and his men are trying to taste the fruit you adamantly told me couldn't be touched. What the hell am I supposed to do?"

Burlone sighs with his thumb and forefinger on either side of the bridge of his nose. "Sei, touch whoever the hell you want. Just leave the passion fruit alone. By some miracle, they're both virgins, and I want them to stay pretty for a little while longer. Understand?"

A seething Sei opens his mouth to argue before snapping it closed in fury. We both know it won't do him any good.

"Now, let's get back to business, shall we?" Burlone states.

Sei's nod is jerky, almost robotic before he rummages through his pockets and pulls out another cigarette. Once it's lit, Burlone continues, "Dex, how are the fruit doing? Any issues?"

"Do we have any clothes for them? If they're not going to be sampled then—"

"Now you think they need clothes? They're whores, Dex. Get it through your fucking skull!" Sei shouts.

Burlone lifts his hand, immediately silencing Sei before addressing me. "Sei's right, Dex. You need to stop looking at them like human beings. Hell, I was generous to leave them with their underwear. Look at them like fruit in the grocery store. Some are a little more round. Some have a few bruises but still promise a sweet flavor. Some have been dropped on the floor too many times and are rotten on the inside. But all of them are fruit, and none of them need clothes. Understand?"

My heart is pounding against my ribcage as both sets of eyes turn to me. With my hands clenched at my sides, begging for a fight, I barely restrain myself from shredding both of the sick assholes in front of me. It takes every ounce of discipline I possess to unfurl my fingers and grit out, "Yeah. I understand."

"Excellent. We have a photoshoot for them next week. Make sure they're presentable and not so damaged that it affects their likelihood of being sold. Now, Sei, how's our little friend doing?"

"Kingston?" Sei sits forward and rests his elbows on his knees with a satisfied gleam in his eye.

"Yeah."

"He's good. And by good, I mean miserable. Sent one of his goons with the girl to get her shit from her apartment. I'm going to assume they'll be shacking up from now on so he can keep an eye on her. Saw them talking to the homeless guy in the parking lot. Handed him a business card in case he sees anything fishy happening around her place."

"Good. Anything else?" Burlone prods.

"Nope. I think that's about it."

"Then you're dismissed." I'm out the door within seconds, stalking toward my room like it's my own sanctuary. One where I won't be able to hear the women screaming as they're taken over and over again.

Squeezing my eyes shut, I turn in the opposite direction and head to the gift shop. Burlone might've said no clothes, but he didn't mention blankets.

CHAPTER FIVE

LITTLE BIRD

I'm going insane. I can't handle this. The isolation. The cold. The creaking pipes. All of it. I'm so exhausted and would kill for some sleep, but I don't dare touch that mattress. Its presence is already enough to give me hives. I can't imagine lying on it to get some rest.

I've been pacing the floors, jiggling the door handle, searching the bed frame for a loose screw––anything to get me out of here.

But they aren't stupid.

I'm stuck. And it scares the hell out of me.

At the muffled sound of keys, I turn to the door to see it swing open, revealing Dex. The only guy I've really seen or talked to since I was brought to this room.

"Hey." He lifts his chin in greeting before putting a tray on the bed. "Brought you some food and a blanket."

Hesitantly, I watch him, but don't take a step closer to the gifts he's placed in my cell. My stomach grumbles at the sight of the food, even though it looks less than appetizing.

"It's soup and a roll," he offers, motioning to the food.

"I can see that."

"Are you hungry?"

"Is it poisoned?" I counter.

With a teasing smile, he tells me, "No offense, Little Bird, but if we wanted to kill you, I don't think we'd need to use poison to do it."

Good point.

My bare feet make scuffing noises against the concrete in the otherwise quiet room as I step closer. When I reach for the soup, I can feel his eyes on me. Clearing my throat, I look toward him and ask, "I'm sorry, but do you need to watch me eat?"

"Sorry." He shrugs. "Boss's orders."

"You don't look very apologetic," I point out before lifting the spoon and bringing it to my mouth.

My nose wrinkles as soon as it touches my tongue.

"Sometimes, it's easier to be indifferent in this business, Little Bird. Is there a problem with the soup?"

"It's cold."

His hand grips the back of his neck, and he has the decency to look sheepish. "Yeah. Sorry about that. Didn't really want to get third-degree burns from one of you throwing your bowls at me."

My mouth tilts up in the corner.

"Good point," I mutter under my breath. Taking another bite of soup, we sit in silence until I'm almost finished and gain the courage to voice a question that's been driving me mad. "Can I ask you something?"

"Yeah," he grunts, eyeing me warily.

"Why'd you take me?"

"I didn't take you."

Bullshit.

"Okay, why'd your *friend* take me? Why'd your *boss* take me? Why am I here?" I ask, feeling frustrated. "I'm a nobody, Dex. I don't understand."

He almost flinches when I utter his name, but I don't comment on it. I need answers. And I need them now if I have any hope of getting out of here.

"No offense, but most of the time, girls like you are taken *because* you're a nobody," he explains.

"What does that mean?" I notice I'm shivering and start rubbing my hands up and down my arms. I'm still only wearing his shirt that he left a day or two ago, but it doesn't help much with warmth.

"It means that in most cases, if we thought someone was going to miss you, then we would've left you alone. In this business, it's best not to draw attention to ourselves."

"What do you mean, *in most cases?*" I press, practically begging for answers.

His lips are pulled into a thin line, and his gaze narrows as he almost stops himself from giving me an answer.

"Please," I beg. "I'm going crazy in here. I need the truth."

I watch as he releases a slow breath then looks at me. "In some cases, you--or someone you know--pissed off the wrong guy, and you're taken as leverage, or sometimes to teach them a lesson with no intention of ever being returned."

Which is exactly what I'm afraid of. But if they don't

know the truth, then I might actually have a chance of getting out of here.

Steeling my shoulders, I push, "So what am I?" I need to know who I'm dealing with. *What* I'm dealing with.

He drags his fingers through his short, dark hair before gritting his teeth and telling me, "You're a little bird who's desperate to be set free from her cage."

Standing from the edge of the bed, he takes a step toward the door when I stop him. "And what are the chances of that happening, Dex?"

He shakes his head but doesn't turn around. The muscles in his back are tense as he utters, "Don't count on it, Little Bird. Not everyone is meant to fly."

And with that, the door slams behind him, and I scream in desperation.

CHAPTER SIX

DEX

"*B*oss wants to see you," Sei says with his shoulder pressed against the wall.

"Boss is out," I reply. "He's at a dinner. Dante's driving."

Sei's face remains blank, but he doesn't bother to cover up his bullshit lie. "You look tired," he notes, trying a different tactic. "When was the last time you slept?"

"Do you need something, Sei?" I ask in an attempt to get to the point. I'm not in the mood for his bullshit, especially after my conversation with Little Bird. Something sparked inside of me, and I need to bury it.

Shrugging, he pushes himself off the wall and swaggers toward me before pulling out a cigarette.

"Just figured I'd check on the fruit. That's all."

"They're fine," I grit out.

"But are you fine? Like I said, you look tired. I'm only looking out for you."

Snorting, I quip, "I'm sure you are. Get out of here, Sei. You're not needed down here."

"I'm not so sure about that." Towering over me from

my seated position in a metal folding chair, he puffs out some putrid smoke. "You see, some of the men have been complaining that you've misunderstood Burlone's orders."

"Is that right?"

"Yeah. They say you've kind of taken the fun out of fruit picking."

"Oh, really?" My mouth quirks up on the side. "That's a shame."

"It is. You see, you've always been a lone wolf. I get that, Dex. Hell, I appreciate it. But now you're pissing off my pack."

"I was given orders—"

"I know your orders," he bites out, pissing me off. "And I also know that you weren't asked to protect all of them, so stop trying to play the hero, or I'll have no choice but to—"

"To what?" Standing to my full height, I puff out my chest and tilt my head a few inches closer to get up in his face and to showcase my point. Sei might be big and bad to everyone else, but he's not Burlone's muscle. He isn't feared like I am. He's Burlone's little weasel. Without the gun on Sei's hip and his perverted ideology that coincides with the Allegretti family, Sei would be useless.

I have to give him credit, though. He doesn't back down. Shoving me in the chest, he keeps his voice low. "I'll have no choice but to tell Burlone that his men aren't happy that one of the job's biggest perks is being threatened by his goon."

"You think Burlone will be happy if the fruit spoils?" I push back.

"I think Burlone doesn't give a shit about the apples,

yet you're treating them all like passion fruit. Give my men—"

"They're not *your* men."

With a smirk, Sei looks up at me with his beady eyes. "I think you'd be surprised."

My forearm is pressed against his windpipe before my mind can catch up with my actions.

Sei doesn't even blink, though his face turns red from lack of oxygen. When I finally relieve the pressure, he coughs. "Let them have their fill of all the other fruit, and they won't touch your passion fruit."

"And if I don't agree to that?" I ask, my hand clenching at my side.

"Then it'll be interesting to see which ones make it to the tournament without any damage. You forget, Dex. I was the one who brought them here. I was the one who saw how sweet and ripe they were for the picking. In fact, I think it might be fun to take a small bite of each of them, just so they remember what it's like to be eaten alive by a real man—"

My fist connects with the side of his face, and his head goes swinging to the left.

Shit, that felt good.

Pressing my full weight into Sei's neck one last time, I crouch lower until my breath fans across his face. "Be careful how you threaten me, Sei. You might think I still have a heart, but it's long gone, and I've lost any shred of mercy that I might've had under different circumstances. You touch the passion fruit, and you deal with me. Now get the hell out of here before I don't give a shit about how much it pisses Burlone off when we fight."

I release the pressure and watch the rage in his eyes

take over until he's vibrating with it. Then, like a chameleon, it dissipates. Cocking his head to the side, he gives me a slimy smile then walks to the closest door that doesn't belong to some passion fruit's cage and shoves it open.

"Hello, Apple," he greets the girl locked inside the room. I've only seen her once. There isn't anything particularly special about her. In fact, I'm not sure I'd even bat an eye if I saw her on the street, but that doesn't mean she deserves the hell Sei's about to inflict on her. The door closes with a loud thud that shakes me to my core. And all I'm left with is the knowledge that I pissed off a rabid weasel then let him loose on an innocent hen.

CHAPTER SEVEN

LITTLE BIRD

*T*he sound of low voices in the hallway wakes me from my restless sleep. Staying in my crouched position in the corner of the room, I listen for anything distinct, but it's too muffled to make out what they're saying.

Seconds later, something slams against the door. Hard. I jump back and press into the rough cinder block wall. My breathing is staggered as I wait to see if whoever is on the other side of the door will go away, or if my nightmare will finally come to fruition in this awful place, and I'll be used like a freaking object. I'm shaking like a leaf when the door squeaks on its hinges to reveal a dark, shadowed figure. When I see Dex's face, I release the breath I'd been holding, but it doesn't stop my quaking.

"You okay, Little Bird?" A cautious Dex assesses me in my corner.

Currently, my knees are tucked into my chest with my arms wrapped around them, hugging them close as I peek up at him. I don't move a muscle, but he can read the terror written on my face, regardless.

With as much reassurance as he can muster, he adds, "They're not going to touch you. As long as I'm here, you'll be safe. Okay?"

"Is that what the loud noise was? Someone wanted to get in here?"

His silence is loud enough to answer my question.

"And what about when you're not here?" I ask, licking my chapped lips.

I watch as his gaze falls to the ground, but he doesn't say anything. I guess he doesn't really need to because we both know the answer.

"Get some rest, Little Bird. I'll be right outside your door."

There's something about the way he says it. The resolution to my depressing future that's mixed with a little bit of defiance too. Like maybe...just maybe...he might be willing to keep an eye out for me while I'm here. And I need all the allies I can get.

CHAPTER EIGHT

LITTLE BIRD

*T*he next time he comes, I'm ready. I've been pacing the room with anticipation, but it doesn't stop my heart from jumping into my throat when the door opens, and Dex appears with a bottle of water in hand.

"Hi." I smile awkwardly, and Dex's brows furrow. "How are you today?" I continue, trying to make small talk. The casual greeting feels foreign and...strange. Especially for our situation.

With a dry laugh, a confused Dex cocks his head. "What's your angle? Why are you acting weird?"

I guess I shouldn't be shocked that he's calling me out like this. Subtlety has never really been my strong suit. Apparently, it isn't his, either.

Taking a deep breath, I begin the monologue I've been practicing since we last spoke. "Okay, so here's the thing. From our last conversation, I learned that I'm not going to be set free. It sucks, but I appreciated you being straight with me. I also learned that if you're around, then I should be somewhat safe. For now, anyway. I guess my first question is, what about the other women I met the first night I came? The ones who were in Burlone's office? Are you supposed to keep them safe too? Or are you only really watching me because I turned out to be a virgin? I assume you make more money from girls who are...you know," I hedge. "*Innocent.*" My nose wrinkles in disgust before I press forward. "That's what the doctor was checking for, wasn't it? When he examined all the girls after we were asked to strip down to our underwear?" I shudder at the memory of the doctor touching me when I was first brought here but push it away and wait to hear Dex's response. Now isn't the time for a walk down memory lane. I need answers, and I need them sooner rather than later if I have any chance of surviving this screwed up situation.

Dex blinks slowly but doesn't confirm or deny my suspicion that he knows more than he's letting on, so I press forward. "Okay then...I guess we'll save that specific topic for a different day. I also made a decision about *you* during our last conversation."

"And what's that?" he asks, attempting to hide his interest with a bored tone.

"I think you seem like a relatively good guy, despite your current occupation choice, which is why I want to ask you something else. You didn't answer me the first time, and I think it's because you were afraid I'd have a breakdown if you told me the truth. But I think that's what's been driving me crazy. The unknown. So, here it goes." I take a deep breath. "What's going to happen to me, Dex? I'm going to assume your boss is biding his time until he figures out what to do with me. Am I right? Has he made any final decisions about my future? I want to know what the possibilities are. I want to mentally prep for any of the possible outcomes that I'm going to have to deal with. Do you think you can help me do that?"

His shoulders deflate right before my eyes, and it doesn't exactly give me warm and fuzzies.

"Tell me," I push, a fresh wave of anxiety pulsing through me. My hands toy with the long white sleeves of the shirt Dex gave me the first night I showed up here. I fist the fabric and pray he'll give me some insight that I desperately need. "Please."

"Little Bird, you seem like you're in a pretty good mood, all things considered, and I really don't want to mess with your day."

"And I get that," I admit before crossing my arms to hide how badly I'm shaking. "But what I think you don't understand is that the *not* knowing is what's driving me insane. If you could just fill me in, then I think I'll be better. I'll be mentally prepared. It'll help me," I reiterate.

"Trust me, Little Bird. I don't think you can mentally prepare for what you're probably going to go through." His face sours as if he doesn't want to think about it, either.

"What's that supposed to mean?" I ask, feeling a sense of hesitation for the first time since our last conversation.

"It means that you've been dealt a shit hand. That's what it means."

"Yeah, but knowing your hand is better than betting blindly, right?" I counter.

With a narrowed gaze, a grudging Dex hesitantly agrees with my logic. "I suppose."

"Then tell me. Please?" He's close to caving. I can see it in his eyes.

After a few long seconds, he mutters, "Honestly?"

I smile. "Yeah. I think it'd be best if we were honest right about now."

For once, I'm not hunched in my corner. I'm standing, stretching my long legs, and realizing how tall Dex really is. When I look him up and down, I notice he's built like a freaking bear. All muscles and tattoos and dark, short hair. Even a blind woman would be able to feel the sexual pheromones he exudes when he's in the room. I just can't understand why he's in this business when it's easy to see that he could have any woman he wants. But I push those thoughts aside. I don't have time to question his motives. Not when I'm so close to getting the answers I desperately need.

Dex clears his throat then takes a tentative step closer. "You're either going to be purchased by a stranger and used as a maid or sex slave, or you'll be used as a buy-in chip for a poker tournament my boss is putting on."

My brows furrow, but I'm more confused than scared. "Huh?"

He laughs, staring at me. "Who are you, and what have you done to the terrified little girl from a few nights ago?"

I join in with a soft giggle, shocking the crap out of both of us. The sound is so foreign to my ears that I take a second to look around and see if the *old me* is in the room. Nope. Just tainted ol' me.

"She's still in here," I admit quietly. "But last night helped me gain a little perspective. I think if there's any chance of me surviving this, then I need to have the full

29

picture. And I think you can explain it to me. Now, can you please explain to me what the buy-in means?"

With a sigh, Dex takes a seat on the edge of the bed, and I force myself to join him, though my movements are jerky and robotic. But if I'm wanting him to talk to me and tell me what he knows, then I need to show him I don't think he's as much of a monster as the rest of them. Sensing my hesitation, he leans away from me and leaves a few inches of space between our legs to keep our thighs from touching. I appreciate the sentiment. It further proves my theory. That he doesn't want to use me like the men on the opposite side of that door. My eyes shoot to it before I force my attention back to the bear beside me.

Dex starts, "In order to enter the tournament, you need to put a woman on the line. If you win, you get to keep yours, along with collecting everyone else's who participates in the tournament. If you lose, then you lose the girl you brought, along with any money you gambled away during the night."

"I–I'm sorry," I stutter, convinced I've heard him wrong. "Is it common for people to have women lying around that they can use for a poker tournament?"

He snorts at my half-joke then answers, "Not always. If you don't, then you can purchase one before the event."

"And where would you purchase one?"

"From someone like my boss." Giving me the side-eye, I finally understand where he's going with this.

"So...even if I'm not used by your boss personally, there's a big chance that one of his *friends*"—I spit the word out, though it still leaves a bitter taste in my mouth —"has the opportunity to buy me from him and use me to get into the tournament. Is that what you're saying?"

"Yeah. I think you pretty much summed it up."

He has the decency to look apologetic, losing his indifference from the last time we talked. I appreciate the sincerity even if it doesn't help my crappy situation. Another wave of anxiety runs through me, so I stand up and bounce on the balls of my bare feet, searching for a solution.

"I suppose there isn't much of a chance that nice guys participate in this tournament, is there? Someone who wears shining armor and rides white horses?"

Shaking his head, he chuckles deep and low. "Don't count on it. And even if there was one, the odds definitely wouldn't be in his favor."

His comment makes me pause. "What do you mean?"

"Burlone is pretty much unbeatable. I've only seen it happen once, and even then, I'm not sure it wasn't entirely a fluke. I've been around for a long time, and I can say with confidence that if I were a betting man, I'd put my money on Burlone. I'd be a fool if I didn't."

"So, if that does happen, and Burlone does win, does that mean I end up right back here? With you?" I swallow, surprised the question spilled out of me. Shifting my gaze to the floor, I try to ignore the way my face heats to a million degrees while I wait for his response.

When Dex stays silent, I peek over at him only to see his entire body filled with regret, and I know I'm not going to like the answer he tells me.

"I'm afraid not, Little Bird," he admits. "If Burlone ends up winning you back, he'll only turn you around for more profit."

I was right. That's a crappy answer, and it leaves me floundering. I never thought I'd admit this to myself, but I just want to go back to my life before this. My life that might not have been rainbows and butterflies, but it was mine, and even though it felt like a prison at the time, I had a hell of a lot more freedom than I do now.

Dex gets up to leave, but I stop him. "Can I ask you something else, Dex?"

"Yeah," he answers gruffly. I can tell he doesn't want to, but he's man enough to hold my pointed stare.

"Have you ever purchased someone?"

If he says yes, it'll kill me. Right now, his visits are the only thing giving me a shred of hope, and if I find out he's nothing but scum like the rest of the assholes in this place, then I think it might break me. In fact, I know it will.

With a shake of his head, he whispers, "Never. I don't think a person should ever be bought or sold. If you ever own someone, it's because they've given themselves to you freely, and they own you too. It's mutual. And it's built on trust. What we do here?" He grits his teeth in distaste. "It's slavery in its lowest form. Goodnight, Little Bird."

He leaves the untouched water bottle on the mattress then closes the door behind him with a soft click, yet his words play through my head for the rest of the night.

CHAPTER NINE

LITTLE BIRD

*W*ith my head resting against the wall, I start to doze after another boring day in isolation, only to hear the hinges squeak.

My eyes pop open, my heart jumps in my throat, and adrenaline spikes in my veins.

Then I see Dex. The sight instantly calms me.

Tucking my knees to my chest, I stay huddled in my corner and fight the urge to greet him like I would a friend.

"Hey, Little Bird," he calls after closing the heavy door behind him.

"Hi," I squeak. My voice is rusty from lack of use. I only ever talk to him.

As if he can read my mind, he gently tosses me a new bottle of water, and I drink it up greedily. Wiping my mouth with the back of my wrist, I tell him, "Thanks."

"Don't mention it."

His hands tucked into his slacks, Dex rocks back and forth on his heels, and an awkward silence encompasses us. It's weird. I haven't felt like this around him since the night we met.

"What's wrong?" I probe, my protective walls rising. Something doesn't feel right.

I watch with trepidation as he clears his throat and looks toward the cold cement beneath his feet. "I'm going to need you to come with me, Little Bird."

"Why?"

His mouth is in a thin, firm line before he swallows hard and gives me a sharp look. "Don't make this harder than it has to be. Please." The slight break in his voice makes me scramble back to my huddled position.

No. No. No.

"What are you talking about, Dex? I need you to tell me what's going on. Remember? We've talked about this. I'll be able to handle crap better i-if I know what I'm getting into. *Please.*" Now it's my turn to beg.

Cautiously, he steps around the bed then offers his hand to help me up. He's never touched me before, and I hate how quickly I give in to letting him. When his giant palm nearly swallows mine whole, I can't ignore the goosebumps that spread up my arms.

It's just because I haven't been touched in so long, I tell myself, wanting to roll my eyes at how pathetic I feel.

That's what isolation does to you, though. It makes you crave human contact more than your next breath.

My legs are shaky by the time I finally make it to my feet, and Dex wraps his arm around my waist to keep me from falling back on my butt. "Careful there, Bambi. You okay?"

I nod, almost laughing at the normalcy of his teasing

before remembering the ominous tone he used moments before.

Peeking up at him, I admit, "You're kind of freaking me out, Dex. You've never taken me outside this room before, and I'm pretty sure it's not to break me out of here."

A dry, helpless laugh escapes him as he drops his head back and looks up at the ceiling while standing almost chest to chest with me.

"I wish." Dex looks down at me and adds, "We're taking pictures of all the girls today."

"All the girls? As in...the ones from my first night here? How long has it been?"

"A week," he grunts. "And the pictures are taken individually. You won't be seeing any of those girls unless they attend the tournament."

He hasn't lost his cool demeanor, so I ask, "Why are you acting weird?" My brows are pinched in confusion because pictures don't seem very terrible. "That doesn't sound too painful, right?"

"I'm going to need the shirt back."

"But—" *Oh.* "And I assume me politely declining your request would be a no-go, right?"

Dex looks like he's about to puke. His skin has lost all its color as he takes slow, steady breaths. "Sorry, Little Bird. But I'm going to need you to cooperate, okay? *Please.*"

It's the way he says please that makes me comply. I don't know why, but he looks closer to crumbling than me right now, and I can't let the big, strong man in front of me break on my behalf. So, I do the only thing there is to do. With shaky hands, I slowly start unbuttoning the dress shirt he had thrown at me the first night we met.

When my knuckles brush against his chest, I recognize how close we're standing and nearly choke on the oxygen as it gets lodged in my throat from surprise. I flinch but don't step back and am surprised when he doesn't either.

I feel like we're in a sick game of chicken as I reveal a little more of my skin, inch by inch, while my captor hovers less than a foot away and watches my every move. When the front is fully opened, revealing my cleavage, stomach, and every inch of my legs, I ask with a trembling voice, "Can I keep my bra and underwear on?"

"Yeah." The word is spoken low and almost sounds animalistic with its harsh rumble. But somehow, it fails to penetrate the tension building between us.

Running on pure adrenaline, I nod, sliding my arms out of the sleeves and handing him the dirty fabric. I haven't showered in days, and I know I stink. My hair is a snarly mess hanging down my back, but I've never felt more desirable. And the hesitant want churning in my lower stomach is what scares me the most.

It's not normal. *So* not normal.

Dex clears his throat before reaching into his suit jacket and retrieving a set of handcuffs that are similar to the ones chained to the bed frame.

"I'm going to need you to put these on, Little Bird," he orders.

"What?"

With a sigh, he grabs the back of his neck before explaining, "I like you, but I'm not a good guy, remember? What you're going to have to go through for the next thirty minutes might be a little rough. I promise I'll do my best to protect you, but you need to listen to everything I say."

"I will." The implicit trust is deafening.

"I'm going to seem cold to you out there." He lifts his thumb over his shoulder, pointing to the door. "I'm going to be harsh. I'm not going to be the guy you've seen every time I come into your room, but it's for your own protection. It's for both of ours." He laughs before sobering. "Understand?"

Releasing a slow breath, I lift my arms and offer my wrists to him, but I don't say a word.

The cold metal is biting as he locks the cuffs around my forearms, making sure to leave them loose, which only proves to me how warped his views are of himself. Dex is a good guy. He just does crappy things and doesn't know how to stop.

After securing the handcuffs, he gives them a gentle tug through the center chain that connects my shackles before guiding me through the door and down the hallway.

I don't really remember the last time I was here. In fact, I'm pretty sure I was still drugged because the memories are insanely fuzzy, but the foreboding unknown mixed with overwhelming anxiety is a familiar concoction that I wish I weren't so accustomed to.

Muffled noises that sound almost like sobbing are coming from a couple of the doors, but I can't quite put my finger on what the sounds are. I'm not sure I want to figure it out, anyway. My head snaps to my left when I hear the distinct sound of a blood-curdling scream that makes my stomach knot. I thought I had it bad, but I know that whatever is going on behind that door is something that nightmares are made of. Dex tugs me a little farther down the hall, and I'm grateful for the reprieve from the screams.

I take a closer step to Dex and almost trip on his heels in search of protection when I place the rhythmic thumping coming from behind another door on my left. The acidic taste of bile floods my mouth, and it takes everything inside of me to swallow it back down instead of spewing the bottle of water I drank a few minutes ago all across the hallway floor.

I never thought I'd feel this way, but I want to go back to my room. *Now.*

There are a few men scattered throughout the hall leering at me as my fingers graze the back of Dex's white button-up shirt. I can almost read their minds, and I hate it. It feels like they're painting me with an oily brush, leaving a film against my skin I can't get rid of.

Sensing my unease, Dex mutters under his breath, "Keep walking, Little Bird. Let's get this over with."

He opens the door at the end of the hall and gently shoves me inside with a look of indifference that's so unlike him, it makes me queasy.

The room is similar to mine, with the exception of two tripods set up in the center of the space. One holds a digital camera; the other appears to be a webcam with a little red light that's blinking away.

With a look over my shoulder, my terrified gaze searches for Dex, who's the only form of comfort I have in this place. I find him lazily leaning against the doorway, looking at his phone without a care in the world.

"Umm…Dex?" I whisper as my eyes dart around the room.

"The photographer will be here in a second. Be a good little girl and stay quiet, yeah?"

My eyes widen in surprise. *Wow.* He wasn't kidding about acting like a jerk. At least he warned me, or I'd be even more terrified right now. Doesn't stop me from glaring at him, though.

"Jackass," I curse under my breath.

After rubbing the palms of my hands against my arms the best that I can while being handcuffed, I pull them into my chest in an attempt to contain my body heat. I feel frozen to the bone from Dex's cold response, along with the draft in the air. It'd help if I had some freaking clothes on. But, no. The chauvinistic pigs haven't deemed me worthy of any.

When the door opens to reveal a strange man with long, greasy hair that smells like smoke, my spine turns into a steel rod, making me stand up straight when all I really want to do is cower.

"Well, aren't you a pretty little piece of fruit," he compliments with a wicked grin.

"Sei," Dex growls. His phone is seemingly forgotten as he pushes off the wall he'd been leaning against. "What the fuck are you doing in here?"

"The photographer needed to take a piss. Figured I'd offer a helping hand," Sei tosses back, though his gaze stays glued to me. He stalks closer. The movement makes the hairs along my skin stand on end, and my fight or flight instinct rushes to the surface.

Closing my eyes, I feel him circle me slowly, inspecting me like I'm a piece of meat at the market instead of a human being. That's when I realize something. This man puts the others in the hallway to shame and is an entirely different caliber of despicable.

When a finger brushes against my shoulder, I shy away from the touch and open my eyes wide in search of my protector. The one who's standing idle a few feet away with clenched fists. He doesn't see me staring at him, though. He's too busy glaring at the stranger's hand like he wants to break it as it skims across my bare skin.

Sei grins at me, showcasing his stained teeth. "Sensitive too. I like that."

"Sei," Dex barks. A silent warning.

"Hey, Dex. Burlone wants to see you in his office. I'll watch over the passion fruit 'til you get back."

The possibility of Dex leaving me alone with this psycho is enough to give me a heart attack. The thought alone makes my palms sweat, and my feet itch to run in the opposite direction.

Dex takes a deliberate step closer but doesn't intervene Sei's perusal as he murmurs, "Sorry, Sei. Burlone told me to stay with her, remember?"

"That's interesting because he told you to stay with the other passion fruit too, and her door's been left unprotected on multiple occasions. Is someone picking favorites?"

"Burlone will kill you if you damage any of the fruit, Sei. I shouldn't have to remind you of that."

"And I shouldn't have to remind you that they're *fruit* in the first place, now should I?" he counters darkly.

"I haven't forgotten."

"You sure about that?"

Dex doesn't deem his question worthy of a response,

so Sei takes full advantage of his partner's hesitation by turning his attention back to me. The fruit.

Slowly, Sei drags his fingers down my spine, starting at the back of my neck. The movement isn't fast. But it's deliberate. And I know the way he paused at the hook of my bra was a silent warning too. A promise. My knees nearly buckle, but I keep my chin up and focus on a discolored cinder block in the corner of the room. It takes everything inside of me to pretend Sei isn't here and that his ghost of a touch doesn't exist.

"She's strong too," Sei notes. "Don't you think, Dex?"

"I guess. Pity it goes against Burlone's orders to touch her, though," Dex reminds him. From the corner of my eye, I see Dex shrug then return his attention to his phone. I think he's trying a different tactic, but I can't be sure. The indifference is back even though Sei's presence had originally sparked the old Dex to shine through for a few minutes, and I already miss him.

"I can be gentle," Sei argues like a little boy petting his new puppy for the first time.

With a scoff, an amused Dex replies, "No, you can't. I've seen the women when you're finished with them, and I think Burlone will notice the difference."

"God, you're right." Sei leans forward, smelling my hair before almost moaning. "But she's a virgin. Did you hear that? A fucking virgin. Do you know what I would do to taste her? To mark her?"

The way he talks––as if I'm not a foot in front of him–– is eerie. Like I'm literally an object to him. Without thoughts or feelings. Unable to voice my opinion or my objection.

Suddenly, I realize something that I never in a million

years thought would happen. I'm grateful to Burlone for something. I'm grateful he told his men I can't be touched. That he placed me under Dex's protection. Because without either of these things, I'd have been broken within an hour. I can see that by the wicked gleam in Sei's eyes as he looks at me, making my skin crawl.

"So, are we going to get the pictures taken care of, Sei? I got shit to do." Dex sounds as bored as ever, snapping me from my thoughts and pulling my attention from that same discolored cinder block I had found so fascinating moments before. Now, I understand what Dex had meant. Getting my picture taken doesn't seem so innocent anymore.

With a sigh, Sei ends his touch near the hem of my underwear then tugs on the ends of my greasy hair as it grazes my lower back before walking toward the camera and turning it on.

"Smile for the camera, baby," Sei calls. Looking through the lens, he snaps a picture where I'm sure I look more like a deer in the headlights than a human being.

Which is probably exactly what he was going for.

CHAPTER TEN

"*W*hat the hell are you doing here, Sei?" a man calls from the doorway as he assesses the room.

"Just helping get the pictures taken. That's all." Sei raises his palms into the air and steps away from the camera.

"Well, I think I can take it from here," the stranger announces.

With a nod, Sei exits the room but not before looking me up and down one last time, leaving me alone with Dex and the...photographer?

"I'm Frank. Nice to meet you." He offers his hand, acting the polar opposite from the asshole who just left, which only amplifies the warning bells going off in my head. At least Sei owned up to being a sick and twisted bastard. This guy seems more like a wolf in sheep's clothing. Then again, I'd assumed Dex was the same way. Maybe my danger radar is broken. My attention shoots to Dex. Yup. It's definitely broken.

Still, instead of taking Frank's hand, I eye it warily as if it's a deadly viper waiting to strike. My lack of response only seems to amuse him.

"I'm not here to touch you," he explains. "I'm here to make you look beautiful. Men spend more money on girls who look pretty for their pictures rather than ones who already look like death. Understand?"

A lump the size of Texas is lodged in my throat, so I don't bother answering. *Already* look like death, as if it's inevitable.

"Understand?" he pushes, losing a bit of his friendly facade.

I give him a jerky nod.

"Perfect."

Mechanically, he grabs my shoulders and turns me at a forty-five-degree angle toward the camera. Then he walks over and looks through the peephole.

Seconds later, he presses his pointer finger against the button on the right-hand side of the camera, snapping a picture.

"Can you smile for me?"

Every instinct in my body wants me to ask why? What's the point? But I keep my mouth shut. When my face remains blank, Frank's eyes heat with anger, his patience almost evaporating into thin air.

"Hey, Dex?" he calls over his shoulder. His gaze is still glued to me.

"Yeah?"

"Help me out, will you?"

Dex walks over with his hands at his sides. I guess he finally tucked his phone away.

"What do you need?" he asks, disinterested.

Motioning to me, Frank tells him, "I need her to look like she isn't a dead fish."

"And how do you expect me to help with that?" Dex laughs darkly before inspecting me with that same look of indifference.

"Touch her," Frank suggests.

"What?" I watch as Dex's brows pinch together in the center, and I find my mind spinning as I try to comprehend Frank's request too. *What?*

"Touch. Her. Even a look of disdain or terror is better than indifference. Maybe it'll bring some color to her cheeks. Just...touch her. Kiss her. I don't care. Spark some sort of emotion in her. It's not rocket science."

"Yeah, but—"

"Do you want me to call Sei back? She looked terrified only a few minutes ago. I'm sure he wouldn't mind—"

"No," Dex cuts him off, stepping over to me. "I'll help."

"Good."

I don't dare say anything to my captor because Dex and I have an audience with the ability to document our every move. I'm not sure what I would say, anyway. Cautiously, Dex takes another step closer then brushes his finger against my bare hip. My stomach muscles tighten in response, but I don't move away.

"More!" Frank instructs as I hear the familiar sound of the camera clicking.

Dex releases a breath and skims the tips of his fingers along my lower back, following across my hip then to my stomach before softly swirling around my belly button. I quiver under his touch, looking down and watching his rough, tattooed skin touch my creamy, untouched flesh. The ying to my yang.

"This is good. Give me more."

Frank is almost forgotten, and even though I know he's there, it doesn't stop Dex from casting his spell on me. My breath gets caught in my throat as he drags his finger up between my breasts then toys with the straps on my shoulders like a flirtatious lover.

I won't admit to myself that I might like it. I can't. But I also can't hide my physical response to his touch, and I know Frank is eating it up.

Gaining the courage to peel my eyes away from his hand, I look up and find him close. Closer than I would've expected when my focus was solely on his touch. His milk-chocolate eyes are glowing with need. And lust. And heat. And overwhelming want. It almost brings me to my knees. I've never been looked at like this. I've never had the opportunity. I might be in a prison right now, but it's not the first one I've ever had to survive in. To say my brother is overprotective would be a massive understatement, which is why I've never even bothered to get close to a man. But this? This is new. And I don't know how to respond to it. With a gulp, I lick my lips and—

"That's a wrap. She looks good enough to eat. And so damn innocent, it's not even funny." I look over at Frank to see him flipping through the shots he'd just taken on the camera.

"Thanks, Dex. I think this might need to be a new tradition. Have you come melt the panties off all our fruit while I snap a few pictures." He pauses as a triumphant smile stretches across his face, his focus still glued to the screen of his camera. "Seriously, you and I both need a raise for how much more money we're going to bring in for her. She looks like she wants whatever you're willing to give her. Like she's close to begging for it. Our clients would kill to have her look at them like that." Pulling his attention away from the images, he looks up at Dex and adds, "You can take her back to her room now. Thanks again."

We're still standing close; his loafers nearly touch my bare toes. Shaking himself from his stupor, he reaches for the links of chain between my handcuffs. Once his forefinger is hooked around the cold metal, he guides me back down the hall and to my room without saying a word.

The silence is palpable when he frees my wrists a few minutes later. With a gentleness I don't expect, he rubs his thumbs along the tender skin before remembering that I'm nothing but his prisoner.

Taking a deliberate step back, Dex mutters, "I'll bring you a fresh shirt tomorrow, and I'll be right outside the door to make sure no one bothers you." Clearing his throat, he adds, "They usually get a little worked up on picture day, so I want to stay close."

My throat feels like sandpaper when I realize what he's inferring, so I simply nod.

And with that, he steps out of the room, leaving me alone with my conflicting thoughts on the man who's supposed to be my captor but is starting to feel a hell of a lot like more than that.

I'm so screwed.

CHAPTER ELEVEN

*I*t's been three days. Three days of awkward protectiveness that neither of us knows what to do with. Three days of wobbling barriers we've both built, yet feel close to crumbling. And three days of knowledge that her potential future will likely be in the hands of someone else.

And it guts me.

"Hey, Boss," I call out as I rap my knuckles against Burlone's open door.

He waves his hand in the air, allowing me to enter. "What do you need, Dex?"

What the hell am I doing here?

Rubbing my hand against my face, I ask, "I was just wondering if you've heard back from any buyers?"

Burlone snaps his head up from his paperwork and looks me up and down. "And why do you ask? You've never been curious about this side of the business before."

He's right to voice his suspicion, but it doesn't stop me from bristling. "I've never been involved in *any* of this side of the business before. I figure if you're giving me the responsibility to watch over the passion fruit, then you're wanting me to transition and take over more responsibilities. Am I wrong?"

It's obvious Burlone believes my load of bullshit by the way he leans back in his chair and steeples his fingers to his mouth. "No. You've always known that you and Sei are my right-hand men. When I retire, I plan on passing my business to one of you. The real question has always been a matter of *who*."

I nod, having heard this before. It's one of the main reasons Sei and I are so competitive with each other. Hell, part of me feels like we're both a couple of mangy dogs fighting over a few scraps that Burlone tosses to us whenever he feels like being entertained. Regardless, we've always known what's at stake because Burlone likes to dangle it in front of us like a couple of damn carrots. Unfortunately, the more time I spend in the basement with Little Bird, the less I know if I want it or not.

"The problem is that you're soft, Dex. But you're smart too. You think of things from different angles that Sei could never dream of. But you're also afraid to get your hands dirty when it comes to the majority of our business dealings, while Sei doesn't have a problem with that aspect. You two make quite the pair. It's a pity you both can't work together without being at each other's throats." He tsks. "However, to answer your question, all of the fruit I had planned on selling will be purchased as buy-ins for the event. Unfortunately, my associates are struggling with payment and are wanting to take care of the logistics on the night of the tournament before it officially starts. Because I'm generous, I've decided to comply with their requests, so we'll be keeping the fruit until then. Are they giving you any trouble?"

My brows furrow. "The girls?"

He nods.

"No. They haven't given me any trouble. The guys, on the other hand, have been little shits who don't know how to *not* touch the merchandise."

Burlone has the audacity to laugh, throwing his head back and slapping his hand against the table before he defends them. "Well, you know how they are. Boys will be boys. As long as they don't touch the virgins, then we're fine. Have you been keeping a close eye on them?"

There are only two. One of which is my Little Bird, though both are gorgeous and hold the same interest from the sorry sacks of shit who want to ruin them. The real problem is that I don't know how to protect them both. I can't be in two places at once, and Sei is making things...*difficult.* Which reminds me....

"Yeah. It wouldn't hurt if you'd remind Sei to back the hell off, though."

With a shrug, an unapologetic Burlone says, "He's trying to screw with you, and it appears it's working. Stop acting like you care so much about the fruit, and he'll stop trying to screw with them. Understand?"

If only that were possible.

"Yeah."

"Good. Now get out of my office. I got shit to do."

* * *

WHEN I SEE Sei heading my way, busy zipping up his pants after exiting a girl's door, I snap.

50

Shoving him against the wall, I place my forearm against his throat and grit out, "What the hell were you doing in there, Sei?"

"Nothing." He has the audacity to smirk.

I shove him harder, praying I bruise his windpipe. "Bullshit. Burlone said you couldn't touch the girls."

With a shake of his head, I release the pressure slightly, and an amused Sei argues, "Who said I touched her? Maybe I just let her watch."

"Back. The fuck. Up." I give him another firm shove before twisting the handle to check on the girl whose room Sei just left.

What I see would break any other man if he weren't raised in this hellhole. Unfortunately for me, it's just another day of the week. And I hate myself a little more for it.

The other virgin, the one I've been ordered to keep innocent, is curled into a ball on the mattress. I approach her slowly and look for any bruising or swelling that marks her exposed skin. But the room is dimly lit, so I'm not sure I'd see it even if it were there.

"Hey," I mutter, inspecting her a little more closely.

Shiiiiit.

Even though I already know the answer, I can't help but ask, "You okay?"

Her eyes are dull and lifeless as she looks up at me from the mattress. She doesn't say a word.

"Answer me, darlin'."

"When's the tournament?" Her voice is quiet. Broken. But not naive.

"Less than a week. Did he touch you?"

She scoffs, tucking her knees closer to her chest as she

lays in the fetal position. "You mean, did he take my precious virginity? Nope."

"I asked if he touched you," I push, finally noticing the angry purple discoloration on her thighs and neck. Marks like these are a dime a dozen at Sin. I've never liked seeing them, and I've never been one to dole them out, either. But ever since my Little Bird landed in my lap, it's opened my eyes to the brutality that is happening right in front of me. Turning a blind eye on the matter and pretending my hands are clean in the process is a bunch of bullshit, but I don't know what I can do to stop it.

"If you have to ask that, then you're dumber than you look," she spits coldly. "Can you go now? I'd like to be alone."

My fists clench at my sides, but I do as she asks and softly close the door behind me. After the hell she's been through, she deserves at least that much. Resting my head against her door, I stare at the one across from me that holds my Little Bird.

If they touched her too....

I'm still pent up with anxiety when I enter, squeezing the doorknob with so much force that I'm positive it'll leave tiny indentations where my fingers were. I know she can feel the tension rolling off me in waves by the way she stands and rushes toward me.

She *never* rushes toward me.

"Are you okay?" The concern clearly written across her face makes my chest ache.

Me? Okay? Did she really just ask that?

I'm her fucking guard, and she cares how I'm doing?

"Yeah." The lie sounds wrong, and I know she can hear it.

"Talk to me. What's going on?" She fidgets with one of the buttons on the fresh shirt I'd dropped off. My shirt. The sight only makes me feel sicker.

I couldn't even give the other girl that much?

Sei's right. I'm a selfish bastard. I picked a favorite. Now, I have to see if I was able to keep her safe when I know I didn't do the same for the other girl.

"Has anyone come in here since I last saw you?" I ask, trying to keep my tone even when I'm seconds away from hunting down Sei and pressing my Glock to his forehead.

With pinched brows, she replies, "No. No one has come in here except you."

"Good." I breathe a sigh of relief and run my hands through my hair as the image from only moments ago haunts me.

"What's wrong?" she presses.

The anguish nearly guts me before I turn to her and admit, "I can't let them touch you, Little Bird."

Sensing my frustration, she raises her hand and gently touches my forearm. Even with the layers of clothes between us, I still find the act soothing. A balm to my soul. And so damn foreign that I find myself frozen in place.

"What happened?" she whispers.

"There's another girl I'm supposed to watch...."

"And?"

"Sei. He got to her." My voice cracks as my Little Bird's eyes gather with tears.

The silence that follows is suffocating. Licking her chapped lips, she blinks a few times, then clears her throat and asks, "I-is she okay?"

"What do you think?" I laugh. "It's all my fault. I

shouldn't have left the basement. I should've stayed here. When I'm down here, they know to stay away."

"It's not your fault, Dex." Her eyes are pleading with me to agree, but I can't.

"It *is* my fault, Little Bird."

"No. It's not," she argues. "You can't control everyone around you. And you can't be everywhere at once, either. Burlone asked you for an impossible task. You're only one man. And they're nothing but a bunch of wolves fighting over—"

"I can't let them touch you," I reiterate, my hands shaking as the real reason for my terror slips out of me a second time.

As a single tear slides down her cheek, she shakes her head sadly. "If something happens to me, then something happens to me. There's only so much you can do."

"How can you say that?" I spit, my frustration bubbling over. "How can you accept your fate like that?"

"I'm not accepting my fate. I'm accepting the possibility that I might be beaten and raped. And probably sold too." With her lower lip quivering, she stands a little taller. "But not that I won't overcome it. There's a difference."

"Not to me. I can't let them hurt you." The desperation is clear in my tone, and instead of arguing, she surprises me. Gently, my Little Bird draws her hand down my arm, then laces our fingers together and brings them to her mouth. I watch the scene unfold in slow motion as she brushes her soft, pouty lips against the back of my hand. Her gaze is glued to mine to show her sincerity as the heat from her mouth brands me with its innocent touch.

But still, she doesn't speak.

And I snap.

"How can you touch me like that? I'm a fucking monster." I go to pull my hand away, but she keeps her hold and surprises me with her strength.

"Dex, I need you to listen to me."

I stop my half-assed attempt to break free and wait for her to spew whatever bullshit helps her sleep at night. Besides, her touch is the only thing keeping me from losing my shit any more than I already have.

"I trust these hands," she whispers. "I trust them, and I trust what you do with them."

Standing on her tiptoes, she softly kisses my temple before dropping back down to the flats of her feet. "I trust this mind and that you're searching for a solution to save me and the rest of these girls, even if you won't admit it to yourself. You know this is wrong, and you want to fix it. I can see it in your eyes every time you look at me."

Lastly, she brings her second hand and places it over my heart as it pounds in my chest. "And this heart? I trust this heart so damn much that it scares me. It's a good one, Dex. Despite the shitstorm you were raised in and taught to believe. It's a good one, and I need you to believe that too."

With less than a few inches between us, I let the intimacy from her words soak into my soul, praying she might be right.

And that's when it hits me. I need to get her out of here. I need to get all of them out of here.

CHAPTER TWELVE

DEX

Sei: Hey.

*M*y brows furrow as I scan the text. Sei isn't exactly known for being chatty, and he definitely doesn't reach out for no reason, which means he needs something from me.

Annoyed, I send my response.

Me: Hey.
Sei: So me and the boys were talking.

I roll my eyes before grudgingly taking the bait.

Me: And?
Sei: And we have a little wager going.

I grit my teeth then send the same message from seconds ago.

Me: And?
Sei: And we wanna know if you spoiled the fruit or not.

This is borderline dangerous. Anything in writing can be traced, and with how closely the Feds are sniffing around, it isn't safe to talk candidly in text. I guess I should be impressed that he's at least still using the code words even though he's always thought they were bullshit.

Me: Why do you ask?

An image pops up seconds later, and the sight makes me squirm. *Shit.* With sweaty palms, I type out another question.

Me: Where did you get that?

As I wait for his response, I pull the image back onto the screen. I hadn't seen it before now. It's one of the pictures Frank took of me and my Little Bird to send to potential buyers. The picture is focused solely on her blazing green eyes as she watches my hand caress the creamy skin on her shoulder, toying with the black strap of her bra. The lust in her gaze is so potent I can still feel its heat nearly branding the back of my hand. The only part of me that's visible in the picture is my forearm, but my tattoo and weathered hands are a stark contrast to her unblemished skin. It doesn't take a genius to figure out that I'm the one touching her.

And Sei isn't exactly a genius.

**Sei: They went out a few days ago. I'm surprised
Burlone let you keep your hand with how adamant he
is about her keeping her virginity.**

Careful, Sei, I think to myself. That text was way too
incriminating for me to justify continuing this conversation. I might deserve to end up in prison for the shit I've
done, but that doesn't mean I want to hand myself over to
the Feds with a big red bow.

Me: If you want to talk, come find me later.

Hitting send, I lean my head against the wall in Sin's
basement. My ass is getting sore from sitting for too long
on this shitty folding chair, but I'm too exhausted to
stand. I'm too emotionally drained to care. Too tense with
anxiety to sleep. Too overwhelmed by my feelings for a
little bird who has way too much trust in me.

When I hear the sound of footsteps echoing down the
hallway, I turn toward the noise to inspect who the
culprit is.

"When I said, *'later,'* I didn't exactly think now," I note,
addressing Sei. His jaw is still sporting a light bruise from
when I punched him. My mouth twitches at the sight.

He saunters over with his hands in his pockets before
pulling out a cigarette and placing it between his lips.

"Maybe I wasn't finished talking." Lighting the cancer
stick, he puffs out a cloud of smoke in my face. I almost
laugh at his immaturity but restrain myself because I
don't want to pick another fight with him. Burlone
doesn't allow fighting between his men, and whether I
like it or not, I still consider myself one of them. Besides,

our last fight was enough to curb my frustration for the time being. However, if he keeps being an asshole, I have no idea how long my renewed patience will last.

"Then talk," I push.

"You fuck her yet?"

My eyes widen in surprise before I school my features to one of indifference.

"Why would you think I would even consider that, Sei? Especially after our little"––I motion to his bruised face––"disagreement. I might do a lot of shit wrong, but I *always* follow orders, which happens to be one of the reasons why Burlone trusted me with the fruit in the first place. Because unlike you, I understand the meaning of restraint."

"The picture says otherwise," he spits.

"Why do you even care?"

"Because I'm sick of Burlone putting you on a damn pedestal and treating you like you're a god. *That's why.* Just tell me the truth. Did you go against Burlone's precious orders? Did you touch her?" Sei is seething. Hell, I'm pretty sure a vein near his right temple is about to burst from frustration. Yet here I am, still sitting in that damn folding chair when Sei takes advantage and tries to intimidate me by crowding me in it. Just like last time.

Casually, I stand to my full height and almost tower over him, but it doesn't stop him from trying to get up in my face. I don't back down.

"Of course, I touched her," I acknowledge with a grin. "You have the evidence in your hand, dumbass. But do you think I *wanted* to touch her, Sei? Maybe you should get your facts straight and ask Frank before you come over here and spout shit you know nothing about. I was *told* to touch her. I was *told* to spark some kind of emotion from her. So I did. Job done. Check. Just another day at the office."

"That's bullshit."

"Is it? Tell me, Sei, have I *ever* shown interest in the girls before? Ever? What the hell makes you think I'd be interested now? You think she's special?" Lifting my arms, I motion to the basement floor where we keep all the girls who've ever been taken by Sei and sold by Burlone.

"Take a look around, Sei. She's a dime a dozen and will be moved to the next place in a week, and we'll all move on with our lives as if she never existed. Now, back off and get out of my face before I make you." My nostrils are flared, and my fists are tight, but I don't move a muscle as I wait for him to decide if it's really worth it to pick a fight with me.

In all honesty, I don't know that I'd win if he chose to escalate this. He's already pissed that I got the better of him the last time we were in each other's faces, and I have no doubt he's chomping at the bit to get his chance at revenge. Sei's known for fighting dirty, and I wouldn't be surprised if he pulled a knife on me to prove a point. But I don't really give a shit anymore. A real fight between us is long overdue. And I'm sick of his shit.

With a misplaced smirk, an arrogant Sei steps back and raises his hands in surrender. "Now, now, no need to get so feisty, Dex. Just wanted to check, that's all. Have a good night."

He saunters back toward the elevator without a care in the world, while I find myself fuming at the lies I had to utter in order to get him to back off.

CHAPTER THIRTEEN

LITTLE BIRD

I'm used to girls screaming now, and I'm used to men's laughter as they discuss their latest conquests. But the baritone shouting? That's *not* normal. Curiosity piqued, I shuffle a few feet closer to the thick, locked door and try to make out the muffled voices.

My eyes fill with tears as soon as they become clear.

"You think I wanted to touch her, Sei? Maybe you should get your facts straight and ask Frank before you come over here and spout shit you know nothing about. I was *told* to touch her. I was *told* to spark some kind of emotion from her. So I did. Job done. Check. Just another day at the office."

Scrambling back like a little sand crab, I push my back into the biting wall and tuck my knees to my chest, holding back the tears that threaten to fall. All the while, that same muffled voice burrows itself into my memory.

I cover my ears and gently rock myself back and forth, feeling more alone than I've ever felt in my entire life. I just want to go home. To go back to the place I hated for so long when I had no idea what real hatred was until this very moment.

I need to get out of here.

My logic battles my fraying emotions as I replay the conversation over and over again. My stomach rolls.

But what hurts the most? He doesn't come to see me.

And I think that's the final straw because it only proves the validity of his comment. It shreds me in two.

* * *

THE NEXT MORNING, I wake up with puffy, swollen eyes from crying only to see Dex hovering near the doorway with a tray of food. I must've been so exhausted I didn't even hear him come in. Apparently, my self-preservation is at an all-time low.

"Morning, Little Bird," he greets me in a gruff voice.

I don't bother to respond.

Sensing that something is off, his brows tug in at the center, and he takes a step closer. When he finds me looking like a mess, his face turns a pale, ashy color. "What's wrong? Did something happen? I had only left for ten minutes. Which asshole was it? What did he look like? I swear to—"

"It wasn't anyone," I whisper, feeling like I swallowed a glass of acid with how sore my throat is.

He kneels down beside me and cups the side of my face with his warm palm. Holding my breath, I have to fight myself from leaning into it.

"Then what's wrong, Little Bird?"

Unable to stop myself, I whisper, "Did you mean what you said?"

"About what?" He searches my face for a hint that might tell him what I'm referring to.

Because I'm a coward, I close my eyes and murmur, "Not wanting to touch me. Being here because you're told to be. Not giving a shit about my future or any of the other girls on this floor. All of it."

Dex literally falls back onto his butt from shock, shaking his head as if he's seen a ghost. The silence is deafening as I wait for him to deny it even though I heard the whole thing with my own ears.

"You really believe that?" he accuses in disbelief.

"It's what you said."

"Yeah, to *Sei.*" Dex spits his associate's name as if it were a curse. "I told you I have to be a different man out there." Raising his arm, he points to the door to emphasize his point. "I told you I have to be cold. Indifferent. Brutal. If we have any hope of figuring this shit out, then I need to stay in their good graces, or they cut me out, and I'm replaced by some asshat who doesn't give a shit that you're an actual human being and not some object to get off on. All those things? I said them for you. Because of you. Because, ever since you showed up, you messed with my head. You made me feel things I have no right feeling. You've made me question my entire way of life, making me feel like a damn fish out of water, gasping for oxygen." With a dry laugh, he leans forward and tilts my chin up to make sure he has my full attention. The simple touch brands me as he continues, "Want to know the ironic part? The more I'm around you, the easier it is to breathe. You're turning into my oxygen, Little Bird, and I don't even know your name."

The truth in his words is enough to break the dam

holding back my fraying emotions since the moment I woke up in Burlone's office. With tears in my eyes, Dex tugs me into his arms, wrapping them around me and gently rubbing my back. I'm not strong enough to fight him. I'm not strong enough to fight anyone anymore. I'm broken. Yet, I'm seeking comfort from the one who threw the final stone that shattered me.

My body wracks with silent sobs as my fingers tangle into the back of his white shirt, trying to get ahold of myself when I finally realize there's no need. Because *he's* holding me. He's keeping me safe. He's being the strong one. He's showing me he's willing to carry me when I'm weak. And right now? Right now, I feel so damn weak.

"Shh," he coos, planting a soft kiss against the crown of my head. I tuck myself farther into his chest, seeking comfort. "It's going to be okay."

My voice breaks. "How?"

"I'll figure something out. I promise."

Squeezing my eyes shut, I tell him a truth I hadn't been willing to admit to myself until this very moment. "Want to know the pathetic thing, Dex? When I heard you...it broke me. I'm relying on you in here, Dex. But I think I'm relying on you in general too, regardless of this room. I think about getting out of here, and it doesn't feel any better because...." I release a shaky breath.

"Because, why?"

"Because I won't have you with me."

With a gentle touch, Dex combs his fingers through my tangled hair, massaging my scalp until I finally gain the courage to look up at him. When I do, he bends down. Slowly. The pace gives me plenty of time to turn away from the opportunity he's pursuing. But I don't. I can't.

I've wanted this since the moment I knew he'd never take it from me without my permission. His breath fans across my heated skin before he presses his lips to mine. The kiss is so soft, so innocent. Yet, I can feel the heat simmering below the surface, and I want more of it. I want it all. I've been so cold and lonely in my prison that I'd give anything to feel his warmth.

Opening my mouth, I graze the tip of my tongue against his lower lip before shifting until my knees are on both sides of his legs. I expect the feel of his slacks against my bare inner thighs to shake me out of this madness, but it only spurs me on. Rolling my hips against him, I place my hands on his shoulders to help me balance.

"You have me, Little Bird," Dex whispers against my neck before snaking his arm around my lower back and guiding my movements. "You'll always have me."

I pause at the promise in his voice. Looking down at the man who swept in and saved me, I decide it's only fair if he has all of me too. My hands fumble with the belt buckle on his pants before sliding down the zipper and reaching for the hard length that was pressed against my core only moments before. Gently, Dex stops me, nearly swallowing my wrists with his hands as he holds me in place.

My gaze snaps up to his, silently asking why he's stopped me when he murmurs, "What are you doing, Little Bird?"

With crimson cheeks, I tell him the truth. "I want you to have me too. I need to give this to you before it's taken from me. I need one moment with you that's all mine that no one can take away. Please—"

Grabbing the back of my neck, Dex cuts off my

pleading with a kiss that burns me to my core, marking me for him and him alone. In the blink of an eye, I find myself on my back as Dex hovers over me. One of his hands is planted on the cold cement floor by my head while the other tugs his pants down and pushes my underwear to the side.

"You sure you want this, Little Bird?" His sincerity weaves into his words as well as his expression.

With a nod, I reach between us and place him at my entrance. I'm done talking. His mouth quirks up in amusement before he leans forward and distracts me with it, teasing me with his tongue. When he presses into me seconds later, I gasp. My breathing is shallow as waves of unfamiliarity wash through me. Wiggling my hips, I try to get used to the intrusion.

"Look at me," Dex growls. His face is pinched in concentration. "You okay?"

The concern in his voice is probably the biggest turn on I've ever experienced in my life, and my need to have him closer flares to life.

"Yeah. I think I am." Still, he doesn't move. He's too busy inspecting me the same way I'm inspecting him. Tiny beads of sweat cling to his forehead from restraint, and I watch in fascination as one rolls down toward his lips. Curious, I raise my head an inch off the ground and lick the salty moisture. The action is enough to snap the last of his self-control.

With rolling hips and messy kisses, I find myself on the brink of oblivion minutes later, panting for some much-needed air as Dex thrusts into me, marking me as his.

A moan slips past my lips, and my toes curl when Dex

finally pushes me over the edge, following right behind me. Groaning deep in his throat, he collapses onto me and tries to catch his breath. I want to laugh when it tickles my neck but restrain myself out of fear that it'll pop the bubble that we've created together. The weight of his body pressing me into the cold cement floor is surreal. And so freaking good.

"I think I liked that," I joke, considering the last thirty minutes of our activities.

"Think?"

"I mean, there's definitely room for improvement. Less clothes, for example—"

Dex blows a loud raspberry kiss to my neck, cutting off my teasing and making me squeal like a schoolgirl. Wiggling against him in an attempt of self-preservation, an unfamiliar set of giggles erupt from deep inside me. Somewhere I didn't even know still existed, and it's all because of him.

So this is what happiness is like.

CHAPTER FOURTEEN

LITTLE BIRD

"So, what's with the tattoo?" I ask, lazily tracing over the black X on Dex's forearm with my finger.

Dex glances down at it. "What do you mean?"

"Well, I assume it means something. Am I wrong?"

He purses his lips before admitting, "No."

"And?"

"It's the Roman numeral for ten."

"And what's so significant about that number, Dex?" I ask as I lift myself onto my elbow and rest my chin against his muscular pec. He's so warm and cozy that I kind of want to just wrap myself around him like a little monkey.

"I was ten when my mom used me to pay off her debt to Burlone. I was ten when I found out I had a father and a brother who didn't want me. I was ten when I saw a man die, and a few months later, was given a gun to do it myself. My entire world was turned upside down, and for better or worse, I think it's the time that I can truly pinpoint and say that it's when everything changed, and I became who I am today."

Schooling my features, I try to keep my shock from showing. "I can't imagine that, Dex. How could your mom do that to you? How could your father and your brother?"

He shrugs, and the action makes me move a few inches up and down as we lay on the cold, hard ground. Neither of us suggested the stained mattress, and I'm totally okay with that. I can only imagine how many haunting memories were created on it, and I don't want them to taint this moment with Dex. When he notices my head bouncing up and down with his shrug, he smiles softly before remembering the shitty topic of conversation I had unwittingly brought up.

"I don't really blame my dad," he admits in a quiet, yet deep voice. "My mom was a prostitute. How the hell was he supposed to believe her? Although, the older my brother and I get, it doesn't take a DNA test to see the resemblance."

A brother. He had mentioned him a minute ago, but I didn't piece it together until now.

Shit.

My blood runs cold as I ask, "So, you know him? Your brother?"

With a nod, an indifferent Dex twirls a few strands of my hair with his fingers. "Not really. I know *of* him, and I've seen pictures. But we don't exactly run with the same crowds."

"Who is he? What's his name?" I try to keep the shaking from my voice, and it appears that post-sex Dex isn't very observant. Or maybe he's just naive enough to believe I'm a random girl off the streets like I wanted him to.

"Diece. Which is ironic, isn't it? Diece means ten in Italian. My name means an order or factor of ten, and my entire world fell apart when I was...." He drags out the word to emphasize his point.

"Ten," I answer for him.

"Ding, ding, ding. We have a winner."

Biting my tongue, I try to keep myself from voicing a question I'm not sure I want the answer to, but it slips out anyway. "I need to ask you something."

"What is it?" he asks as he brushes a stray strand away from my forehead.

"Do you know my name?"

With confusion clearly written across his face, he looks down at me and shakes his head. "You know I don't."

"Are you telling me the truth, Dex?" I press.

He counters with a question of his own. "Why would I lie?"

Shaking my head, I sit up and tuck my knees to my chest in an attempt to protect myself from falling apart. There's no way this is a coincidence. There's just no way.

"What's going on, Little Bird?" he probes before pushing himself up and sitting next to me on the dank floor.

I'm terrified right now. I've been hiding for a reason. I haven't revealed my name because it would only put me in more danger, if that's even possible. But this? Knowing the connection we have? I can't do this to him. I can't lie.

I bite my tongue until the metallic taste of blood fills my mouth.

"Tell me, Little Bird."

The truth tumbles out of me before I can stop it. "I know your brother."

His mouth opens an inch before closing again. Then he looks me straight in the eye as his defenses slide back into place. "What? How?"

"We were practically raised together."

With narrowed eyes, his suspicion spikes. "What's your name, Little Bird?"

Touching my lips and breathing deep, I tell him the truth. The one I've been hiding since he opened my prison door and slid off his shirt to keep me covered. The memory feels like so long ago, yet it's been less than a couple of weeks.

"My name is Regina Romano, the princess of the Romano family. I'm Kingston's little sister, and I've been taken to get back at him for screwing up your boss's plans."

A tense silence fills the air as he registers my words, staring at me as if I'm a ghost coming to haunt him.

Sucking my lips between my teeth and pulling them into a thin line, I wait for him to say something. Anything.

Minutes later, he utters one word while staring me straight in the eye.

"Shit."

CHAPTER FIFTEEN

DEX

"*D*o we have everything in order?" Cigar in hand, Burlone sits behind his desk and asks his question through a puff of smoke.

I stay quiet because I have nothing to do with the tournament. My only job is to keep the fruit from being spoiled. Too bad I failed epically on that one. But he doesn't need to know that. He also doesn't know who he has in his basement. Unless he already does, and I suspect he might.

The real question is, how the hell do I figure out the truth without drawing attention to the fact that I know Little Bird's true identity when Burlone has exhausted so much effort to hide it from one of his closest men. My gaze shoots to Sei. Does he know? Is that why he's so interested in getting to her? I almost laugh. Of course, he knows. He was the one ordered to bring her in. How the hell has he kept it a secret, though? I shake my head as my mind tries to piece everything together. Sei has spent more time traumatizing the other passion fruit than he has with my Little Bird. But why? Maybe it's because he knows her true identity and understands what would happen to him if Burlone found out he spoiled her before his plan could come to fruition. Maybe that's why he's been so focused on the other girl. Because he knows she's a nobody while my Little Bird is the exact opposite.

"As far as I know," Sei offers with a shrug, bringing me back to the topic at hand. "It's not like you tell us much."

Burlone glares, narrowing his eyes. "Want to say that again, Sei?"

Sei has the decency to look bashful, and I don't blame him. Burlone's in a shit mood. And no one is safe from his wrath when he gets like this.

"No, sir," Sei mutters. "I just meant that you only give us pieces to work with but not the whole picture, which makes it difficult for us to know if everything's in order. That's all."

Shifting his gaze to me, Burlone asks, "And how's the fruit?"

"Ripe for the picking." The lie slips past my lips without a hitch.

"Good. And since Sei is feeling out of the loop, would you both like to know a little secret?"

We lean forward in our chairs in the middle of Burlone's office, ears perking up. Is this it? The moment where I find out if Burlone knows who he has in his custody? Or is this the moment when I finally understand his plans for her so that I can figure out how to get her out of it?

"The passion fruit is going to be picked in front of everyone after the tournament finishes." Burlone's twisted

73

laughter interrupts his comment before he can even get the entire statement out.

Sei and I look at each other in confusion before Sei asks, "What do you mean?"

"I mean that we're going to make Kingston watch a group of men take his girlfriend and his sister over and over again before slitting his throat and making them bathe in his blood." With an arrogant smirk, he takes another puff of the cigar, rolling the stogie between his fingers.

My blood runs cold, but I know I need to extract as much information as I can from the sorry sack of shit in front of me even if it makes me sick to my stomach. It's the only hope I have. The only hope *we* have.

Clearing my throat, I probe, "His sister?"

"Oh, did I not tell you that part?" He laughs. "One of the passion fruits. The one who was drooling over you during the photo shoot. She's the Romano princess."

"So you found her then?" I ask, turning to Sei while pretending I didn't know the truth.

Rolling his eyes, Sei puffs out his chest. "Of course, I did. Burlone ordered me to retrieve her. You're not the only one who knows how to do their job, Dex."

"Now, now," Burlone interjects. "Dex deserves a little more credit for not being a nosy sonofabitch. He understands the importance of keeping his head down while focusing on his tasks and his tasks *only*." Burlone's beady eyes shoot to Sei. "You could learn a thing or two on that front, Sei."

Jaw clenching, Sei's earlier amusement vanishes, but he keeps his mouth shut.

"So, you have no intention of letting Kingston leave?" I

ask in an attempt to pull a bit more information from Burlone while he seems to be in an arrogant enough mood to give it to me.

"Of course not."

"Even if he wins?"

Burlone scoffs. "Do you really think that's possible?"

"No." I shrug. "I was just wondering if you'd honor the rules if he performed a miracle and did. That's all. Does anyone else know about your plan?"

"Not yet. I thought it'd be fun to surprise everyone. They all see how weak he is. It'll be a relief for them to finally cut his family line."

That's a load of bullshit, I think to myself. The Romano name is not to be taken lightly, and I don't think Burlone has really considered the possibility of his idea backfiring. Even with Burlone's sizeable backing from multiple cartels and a few other key families who have a problem with the Romanos, taking them on is a death wish. And killing the head of the family while at a sanctioned neutral location? It's ballsy, to say the least. And insane.

Which is exactly what Burlone is counting on while assuming his associates will choose his side over Kingston Romano, and consequently, my Little Bird.

"And the Feds? Anything new on that front?" I probe, even though I can't stand to hear another word. The need to see Regina and figure out a solution is overwhelming, but I fight the urge to run out of Burlone's office and slam the door behind me. Keeping my composure cool and relaxed, I cross my arms over my chest and wait for his answer.

"No. They've been quiet lately. Although, we've been

75

laying low too, so maybe that's why. Have either of you suspected anything?"

Sei shakes his head, and I follow suit.

"Interesting. If either of you hears anything, I expect you to report it immediately. Understand?"

Duh.

"Yeah, Boss," Sei confirms.

"Good." The ash falls from his cigar, landing on his desk before he brings it to his mouth and inhales slowly. Seconds later, he exhales and lets the puff of smoke swirl in the air. "Dex, make sure the women are showered and have clothes. We need them to look presentable for the tournament. Sei, can you please get everything ready for the transport to the sanctioned location?"

Again, we both nod. "Sure thing."

"Good." With a flick of his wrist, Burlone excuses us. "Now, get out of here. And close the door on your way out."

I try to keep my steps casual when a burst of adrenaline pumps through me. I've got shit to do too.

The question is…where do I start?

CHAPTER SIXTEEN

DEX

*W*ith a soft click, the door to Regina's prison closes behind me.

"Hey." An innocent smile tugs at Regina's lips when her eyes flutter open. She's been sleeping more peacefully since we had sex as if her trust in me is absolute. And it's that same blind trust that urges me forward, pulling her into a hug. Her entire body melts as soon as she's in my arms. A soft sigh escapes her lips.

"Mmm...I've missed you," she admits dreamily.

"I've missed you too, Little Bird." I squeeze her a little tighter before remembering how tiny she is. How breakable. Loosening my hold, I mutter, "We need to talk."

Sensing the urgency in my voice, she pulls away and looks up at me. "What's wrong?"

"We can't let you go to that tournament."

"Yeah, I know—"

"No," I interrupt. "You don't understand. We need to get you out of here as soon as possible, and we need to

77

warn your brother that if he goes, he'll be walking into a trap."

Her mouth opens in shock, her eyes wide. I watch as her lips form a small 'o' before releasing a slow breath. "Okay...how do we warn him?"

"I need you to write him a letter." I reach into my back pocket and pull out a pen and paper. "I need you to explain that if he shows up at that tournament, then he won't walk out of it. I need you to tell him that I'm on your side. That I fell for you. That I'm going to do everything I can to save you. I need you to tell him to trust me. Do you think you can do that?"

Her eyes bounce around my face, soaking up every word like a sponge before she asks, "Is that true?"

"Is what true?"

"That you fell for me?"

Shit. I'd been so focused on her safety, I hadn't even realized my feelings for her had slipped out in the process.

Swallowing thickly, I bring her back into my chest and hold on for dear life. "I can't let you go to that tournament."

She burrows into my chest, trembling slightly as she whispers, "What if you can't stop it?"

"Then I'll die trying."

"Don't even say that. I'm not kidding, Dex." Her tone is sharp, her back turning rigid. She's pissed at me for even bringing up the possibility that I might not make it out of this. The irony isn't lost on me. She's fine sacrificing herself for me or her brother, but when it's the other way around, it's unacceptable to her.

She's a brave little shit. I'll give her that.

"Look." I rub her back, trying to soothe her in the only way I know how. "It's not like I want to die. I'm just saying that you going to the tournament isn't an option. We're going to figure this out, okay?"

"But...how?"

A blaring *I have no fucking idea* flashes through my mind before I shove it away and focus on the issue at hand. Swallowing, I present the first step. "First, we need to get your brother this letter. I need an ally right now, and I think he's our only shot."

"Then we're screwed," she admits with a dry laugh. "Kingston will kill you before you get within ten feet of him or any of his men. How are you going to deliver the letter?"

"I have an idea."

With pursed lips, a doubting Regina folds her arms. "Which is?"

"Don't worry about it. All I need you to do is write the letter and hold on while I'm gone for an hour or two."

"Where are you going?" She reaches for the pen and paper before sitting on the floor to use the slab of cement as her own personal table while waiting for my response.

"Out," I offer. "I have an idea of how to reach my brother––*alone*––and I think he's the only one who will give me a chance without shooting me between the eyes. That is if he even knows I'm his brother."

Brother. It's such a foreign concept for a guy like me. Sure, we're blood. But we're also enemies in every other sense of the term. Will it be enough to save Regina? I have no fucking clue.

Regina doesn't answer right away. She's busy concentrating on her letter, and I watch in fascination as she writes every word in swirling cursive across the paper. Even her handwriting is dainty and feminine. It's a stark reminder of how different we are and only makes me want to protect her more.

When she finishes, she pops the cap back onto the pen and folds the paper into a perfect little square before offering both to me.

"Here you go. And I don't remember D ever talking about a long-lost brother. But I do remember my brother making an off-handed comment once or twice about D's dad being an ass for sending someone away instead of bringing him into the fold. After hearing your history, it was easy to piece the information together. Plus, if D sees you up close, I don't think it'll be too far of a reach for him to figure it out, too."

I cock my head. "Do we look that alike?"

"Honestly? When you opened the door to my room that first night I was brought here, I thought you were him coming to save me. After I realized you weren't Diece, I convinced myself that I was still drugged up, and the similarities were minimal, but"—she tilts her head and looks me up and down—"yup. You guys are definitely related."

I nod while a low hum of anxiety pulses through me.

"Good to know. Hopefully, it'll give me a few more minutes with him before he pulls the trigger."

"Don't talk like that," she scolds, her forehead wrinkling.

"Sorry," I mutter, though I don't take it back.

"Are you going now?" she adds, still sitting cross-legged on the floor. I offer my hand, then pull her up and lean forward for a kiss goodbye. I think I'm needing it more than her, but she doesn't hesitate in returning it.

Stepping away, I slip the note into my back pocket and turn on my heel. "I'll be back soon. Be safe."

"I will. Be safe, too. Please."

Tossing a wink over my shoulder, I add, "Always, darlin'."

CHAPTER SEVENTEEN

DEX

*T*he place is as sketchy as I remember it. Same chain link fence that's been cut in a few places, same worn asphalt that needs to be replaced, same cracked sidewalks and graffitied walls. The fact that Ace lived here--by *herself*--baffles me.

Scanning the parking lot, I find the man I'm looking for and walk over to him.

"Hey." I lift my chin in greeting.

The homeless guy looks up at me in a daze before fumbling in his wool blankets.

"You're the guy. The guy I was supposed ta watch out for. What are ya doin' here, anyway? You're not supposed ta be here. Why are you here? And where's that damn card? He told me ta keep track of it and call if ya showed up, and y-you're right here," he continues mumbling under his breath in search of the card that I assume has Diece's contact information on it.

I crouch in front of him and start helping in his quest,

breathing through my mouth when the stench of alcohol and bad breath wafts through the air.

When I find it tucked next to a bottle of bourbon, I pick the business card up and hand it to a very intoxicated old guy that I feel sorry for.

"Here. Is this what you're looking for?" I ask.

He squints his eyes to take a closer look. "Yeah. I think that's it. But why...why are ya helpin' me?"

"Because I need you to do something for me."

Fiddling with the business card in his hands, he wrinkles his nose. "And what's that? I don't think we like ya—"

"*We?*"

"Ace and me. She and that big man told me ta keep an eye out for ya. They told me ta call if ya showed back up. You really do look like him, ya know—"

"Yeah. That's what I've heard. Listen"—I pull out a burner phone then hand it to him—"I need you to call him and tell him I stopped by. I need you to tell him that I gave you a letter from Regina. Do you think you can do that?"

He cocks his head to the side, looking confused as hell. "Regina?"

"Yeah. Can you do that?" I repeat, eyeing him warily. He's drunk off his ass.

Waving me off, he mutters, "Yeah, yeah, of course. Let me sober up a bit first, though. Ace don't like it when I drink."

With pity shining in my eyes, I push the phone into his hand and cover it with my own to make sure he's got a good grip. "I'm going to need you to call him right now. It's to keep Ace safe, understand?"

His gaze clears almost instantly, sensing the gravity of the situation. Nodding his understanding, he attempts to dial the phone number printed on the business card. After his third attempt, I grab the phone and press the correct combination then hand it back to him. "Here."

"Thanks," he slurs, his voice showcasing his embarrassment.

Releasing a sigh, I wait for the call to connect, praying it won't go to voicemail. When I hear a muffled voice echo through the shitty earpiece, I lean closer and try to ignore the pungent smell clinging to the homeless guy.

He clears his throat before mumbling, "Hey, hey, it's me. Ya gave me yer card a few days ago, or maybe it was weeks? But I—"

Someone talks on the other end.

"Yeah, yeah. Anyway, ya asked that I give ya a call if that guy showed back up and—"

The voice cuts him off while the homeless guy starts nodding up and down like a bobblehead.

"Yeah, yeah. He's here. Asked me ta give you a letter. It's about R-R—" He looks at me. "What was her name again?"

"Regina," I finish for him.

"Ah, yeah. That's right. Regina. He's got a letter about Regina—"

The same brash voice interrupts him again, and I lean even closer while holding my breath in hopes of hearing what's being said. Unfortunately, I can't make out what Diece is saying.

Glancing up at me, Ace's friend replies, "Oh, yeah. Sure. He's still here."

After listening to Diece's response, the homeless guy pulls the phone away from his ear and offers it to me. "He wants ta talk to ya."

Shit.

This could go one of two ways. I just need to pray that whatever the hell Regina wrote in her letter is enough to convince them that I'm the good guy. I didn't bother reading it because I assume it's private, and I respect Regina enough to give her an ounce of the privacy that's been missing from her life. However, I'm definitely questioning my decision as I wait to talk with my half-brother while praying he's not going to kill me.

Literally.

Grabbing the phone, I shift it to my other hand before bringing it to my ear. "Yeah?"

"This Dex?" a low voice grumbles.

"Yeah."

"Why the hell are you using Eddie to contact me?"

I scrub the palm of my hand against my face then admit, "Because it was the only way I could think of."

"And *why* are you contacting me?" His tone is cold. Hell, it's frigid.

Gritting my teeth, I explain, "Because you're walking into a shitstorm, and I'm trying to keep you all from getting fucked."

He scoffs, and I don't blame him in the slightest. "And you expect me to believe that?"

"No, I expect you to believe Regina."

"Don't you say her name," he spits. "After the hell you and your boss are putting her through, I don't want to *ever* hear you utter the name Regina again. Do you understand me?"

Pinching the bridge of my nose, I count to ten and pray for patience. "No offense, Diece, but you have no idea what you're talking about. Read her letter. See what

85

she has to say. And help me get the Romano family––and Regina––out of this mess. That's all I'm asking for. That's all she wants. Just...," I sigh. "Just read the damn letter."

A beat of silence greets me, and I look down at Eddie to see him curling back into a ball like when I first found him. I could've ended up like that. Some nobody on the street who's only love is found in a liquor bottle. Instead, I found Regina.

I need to get her out of this mess. And I need Diece's help to do it, which means I need him to listen to me.

"Look—" I start, but he cuts me off.

"If you think I should trust you, then...." He stops to clear his throat—and probably to second guess himself too. "Then stay where you are. I'll be there in ten."

The call goes dead, leaving me on my own while I fight every instinct inside of me that's telling me to run before a bullet meets my skull.

But I don't.

CHAPTER EIGHTEEN

DIECE

The likelihood of me walking into a trap is far from slim, but it doesn't stop me from putting the car in park and turning off the ignition. Tugging the sleeves of my suit down an inch, I walk toward the dumpster where I last saw Eddie. Only this time, a bear of a man is standing next to it. His hands are raised in the air in an attempt to put me at ease as he watches me approach.

It doesn't work.

"I'm still here," he calls out to me when I'm twenty yards away.

"I can see that. I think the real question is, why?"

Not moving an inch, he says, "Any chance you'd be willing to go somewhere private? Where we can talk? I'm getting itchy out in the open."

His comment isn't what I expected, and neither is the way his gaze shifts left and right while scanning the parking lot. Either he's scared out of his mind, or he's waiting for someone to jump out of the bushes and put a gun to my head. I can't decide which.

"And where would you like to go?" I ask cautiously.

"I dunno. Ace's apartment? A diner somewhere?"

My suspicion spikes. "No offense, but I think it's best if we stay here until you can convince me to trust you." *Even though I'm as itchy as you are to get out of this situation.*

With a nod, Burlone's right-hand man slowly starts lowering his arms back down to his sides. "I'm reaching for the letter. Don't shoot me before I have a chance to prove that I'm on your side, okay?"

My jaw is like chiseled granite as I thumb the Glock in my jacket and watch his every move, prepping for any possible outcome. Although it'd be really nice if I didn't have to shoot my own brother today.

Just sayin'.

Seconds later, Dex pulls a folded piece of paper from his pocket just like he voiced and offers it to me.

"Here."

Releasing a breath I didn't know I was holding, I take it and slowly unfold the creased letter.

Hey, King,

It's me. First—I'm so sorry I snuck out. I screwed up, and that's on me. But I want you to know I'm okay. Please don't shoot Dex! He's been watching over me. He's been taking care of me. He's been really good to me, King. He's not like the other men. I know you'd kill me if I were in front of you right now, but I really care about him, and I'm begging you to give him a chance. He wants to get BOTH of us out of this situation and has information from Burlone that the tournament is a trap. I'm sure you've already been able to guess that would be the case, but Dex can confirm it. You can't go. I don't care if I'm sold or...whatever the plans are for me. Burlone is going to kill you if you show up, and I can't let that happen. Especially because if I had listened to you, I wouldn't be in this position in the first place. Just be careful, okay? And listen to Dex. He's the only shot we have.

Love you,

Regina

When I'm finished reading the message for a third time, I look at my brother and tilt my head toward my car. "Get in."

He listens, keeping his hands out of his pockets and within clear view of my suspicious gaze as if he knows I'm still a little trigger happy. Both car doors slam shut with a thud before I turn on the sleek, black sedan and start driving toward King's estate. The awkward silence is deafening, but I don't know what to say. There's more than one elephant in the car with us. Where the hell do I even start?

My fingers tighten around the steering wheel as I ask, "So, is this true? You've been watching over Regina?"

"Yeah," he responds in a gruff voice.

"Why help us? Why tell King he's stepping into a trap when you know Burlone will gut you in the ugliest way possible if he finds out that you're a rat. Why do any of this?"

Dex keeps his attention out the side window, watching the green trees blur across the landscape as we get closer to our destination. "I think we both know I've never really fit in with the Allegrettis."

My head snaps to him. "What's that supposed to mean?"

"I think you know what it means," he mumbles under his breath.

"Spell it out for me, then."

"My father was a Romano. I guess it's in my blood, just like it's in yours." Turning in his seat and looking straight at me, he waits for my reaction.

Shit.

I first suspected he was my brother when his mom drove up and begged for money. A few years later, I confirmed my suspicion when a picture of him standing next to Burlone was found on my dad's desk. And now, as he sits next to me, I know the truth without a doubt.

"How long have you known?" I mutter, my hands still clenched around the wheel.

"A while. You?"

"A while," I repeat with an amused smile. "Why haven't you reached out?"

He laughs. "Because I was already turned away once, Diece. Burlone took me in."

I scoff before he has a chance to finish, and he rolls his eyes at my immature response before clarifying, "Okay, he took my mom up on her offer to trade me for a kilo of cocaine and her debt wiped free. Regardless, he put a roof over my head and raised me. Even if it was a pretty shitty upbringing, at least he did that much. My own dad? He couldn't stand the sight of me."

I squeeze the steering wheel and grit my teeth. He only knows half the story.

Taking a deep breath, I try to explain the other side. "That's not entirely true. He had his own set of issues, okay? But don't let that affect your future. Burlone's a filthy asshole who deserves to have his dick cut off. Or are you too blinded by your history to see that?"

Shaking his head, a low burn emanates from his eyes. "You're right. Burlone needs to be put down, and I'm here to help you do it."

As I watch him from the corner of my eye, I try to figure out if he's telling the truth or not. The only problem is that I'm not a freaking lie detector like Kingston is. I guess only time will tell, and we'll find out soon enough.

Turning into the long driveway that leads to Kingston's house, I let the silence encompass us then shove my car in park once we've reached our destination. Turning off the ignition, I ask, "So, tell me, Dex...if I put my neck out for you, will I regret it?"

Without hesitation, he looks me straight in the eye. "Not a chance in hell."

"Good because I think we're about to find out."

I lift my chin toward the front of Kingston's estate and open the car door before heading inside. Dex follows behind.

CHAPTER NINETEEN

DEX

I feel itchy. It's the only way to describe it. As if a thousand deadly spiders are crawling along my skin, but I've been told that if I brush them away, their tiny fangs will sink into my flesh and fill me with a debilitating poison.

"Wait here," Diece orders when we reach the foyer.

I lift my chin in acknowledgment. "Sure I won't get shot if anyone finds me here without a guide?"

"If we wanted you dead, you wouldn't have stepped a single foot onto our Italian marble tiles," he quips. "I'll be back in a few."

Then he's gone. Rocking back on my heels, I look around the expansive entryway as I realize that this is Little Bird's home. This is what she was taken from. This is where she was raised. I take in the dark banister leading to the second floor where I assume the bedrooms are. Perusing the walls, I search for a family photograph, but they're bare. Not a single slice of evidence can be seen from where I'm standing that Regina Romano ever existed in the first place. I assume it was in an effort to protect her identity from Romano's enemies, but still. Maybe Regina and I aren't that different after all. One thing is for certain. When I imagine a life without her, it nearly cripples me.

The itchy feeling intensifies, pulling me from my reverie. Glancing over my shoulder, I find a guy in a suit studying me from down the hall. He doesn't bother to retreat when I catch him staring. He simply folds his arms and rests his shoulder against the doorframe.

Self-preservation takes over, and I do a quick scan to see a handgun strapped to his chest that peeks out from beneath his suit jacket. I came unarmed to meet Diece because I didn't want him to feel threatened. But right now? I feel naked without my Glock, and I'm afraid the stranger watching me can feel it too.

"Come on in," Diece calls, making me jump while simultaneously ending the little staring contest I'd been having with the guy down the hall.

Pulling my attention back to my brother, I follow him inside what I assume is Kingston Romano's office. It's cleaner than Burlone's. More polished, maybe. The stench of cigar smoke isn't present, though, and the musk that accompanies Burlone wherever he goes is missing from Kingston's office too.

"Take a seat," Kingston offers coolly before dropping his gaze to the chair adjacent to his desk.

"Thanks."

"What do you know about me?" he asks, jumping right into the interrogation. I shouldn't be surprised. He needs answers from me, and he's a master at getting them by any means necessary. Too bad for him, I won't be needing any persuasion today.

"Enough," I respond blandly.

"Enough to know that I'm pretty fucking good at being able to tell if someone is telling the truth or not?"

I hold his stare. "Yeah. I may have heard that."

"Then let's cut the shit, shall we? Did you fuck my sister?"

With a slight flinch at his derogatory term, I answer, "Yes."

He doesn't move a muscle, but I can tell I've surprised him with my honesty.

"Do you care about her the same way she cares about you?" he asks.

I could kick myself for not having read Regina's letter, but I assume she revealed her feelings for me. If anything, they're tame compared to what I feel for her.

"Yes," I answer.

"Am I walking into a trap?"

This is Regina's brother, and it kills me that I have to tell him that if Burlone gets his way, his blood will be on my hands. "Yes."

A stone-cold Kingston rests his elbows on the table as he continues studying me. "Are you willing to betray the Allegretti family by giving us confidential information that, if linked back to you, will guarantee the skin being flayed from your body by Burlone? And that if we find out the information you give us is faulty, then we'll do it ourselves?"

Damn, Regina. Your brother has balls, I think to myself. The fact that he just laid out my likely future without batting an eye proves to me that he deserves all the respect his name demands.

Without hesitation, I answer, "Yes."

"And what do you want in return?"

An image of Regina flashes through my mind. Her hair is still a tangled mess, and the remnants of makeup cling beneath her eyes. But she's smiling. At me. There's so much potential there. All that we could be. All that we could've been. If I weren't a filthy Allegretti and she weren't the princess of one of the most powerful mafia families in the states. I shake my head to disburse all the potential ways Regina and I could've lived our lives if we weren't stuck with the shit hand we'd both been dealt.

Instead, I simply reply, "I want your sister to be safe."

His gaze narrows in suspicion, reading me like a book. "Tell me the *whole* truth, Dex. I told you to cut the shit, remember?"

Bristling, I drop my head back in defeat and stare up at the ceiling. "You want the whole truth, Kingston? Fine. I want her to be safe. But I also want to keep her for myself because she already owns me. I didn't ask for it because I'm not stupid enough to think it's a possibility. I'm a fucking Allegretti who'll be dead by the end of the week as soon as my men find out that I'm the traitor who screwed up Burlone's plans by squealing to the enemy." Dragging my hands from the top of my head and down my face, I bring my gaze back to his. "So, yeah. If I can ask for one thing, then I want her safe. That's it."

"And you're not going to ask for your own protection?" he pushes.

"I'm not naïve enough to think I'd get it, Kingston. I've been in the game long enough to know you never really trust someone who's always been your enemy even when they show up at your front door to help you."

"No. You're showing up at my front door to help my sister. You don't give a shit about me because of what your dad did to you as a kid. Or *didn't* do, in his case. However, you haven't always been an enemy to the Romano family. You're a victim of an old man's wrong decision, and I think we can both come to an agreement—if you're willing to prove your loyalty."

It takes me a second to register his words. My lungs stop expanding, and I hold my breath as I replay his statement in my head. *You haven't always been an enemy. We can both come to an agreement...if I prove my loyalty.*

That's the real question, isn't it? Kingston wants to know if he can trust me. What he doesn't understand is that I'm not doing this for him. I'm doing it for *her*.

Or maybe he does understand, and he's still willing to play along because, despite how badly he doesn't want to admit it, if he wants to get out of this alive, then he needs me. And I need him if I want to keep her safe.

"And how do I prove my loyalty?"

Scratching the five o'clock shadow on his jaw, he tells me, "We'll be in touch."

CHAPTER TWENTY

REGINA

"Hey, Little Bird," Dex greets me, sneaking in through the door.

"Hi." I'm tense, and it doesn't take a genius to figure out why.

"What's wrong?"

"Where were you?" I accuse, my panic finally taking over.

Rushing toward me, Dex opens his arms to hold me, but I shrug away from him. "Answer my question, Dex. Where the hell did you go?"

"I told you—"

"Yeah. You told me you were going to meet with my brother and that you'd be back in a few hours. That was *yesterday*." I emphasize the word as my blood practically boils in my veins. "So, let me ask you again. Where the hell have you been?"

Scanning the empty room, he keeps his tone low and quiet so that I have to strain to hear him. "I met with your brother. Then Diece dropped me back off at our original

97

meeting place. I got a call from Burlone to collect some shit with Sei since I was already out and about. By the time I finally made it back here, Diece called with an update on…"—he drops his voice even lower—"the plan for tonight, and I had to make sure everything was ready and in place. I'm sorry I couldn't come to you sooner, okay? I figured you knew I was doing everything in my power to keep you safe—"

"And possibly getting caught for it!" I whisper-shout. "You scared me half to death! Things have been happening here…."

His face turns pale. "What kind of things?"

Shaking my head, I raise my hands and try to put him at ease. "Not those kinds of things. It's just…I can hear the girls being escorted from their rooms. But they're not coming back. Where are they taking them?"

The realization dawns on Dex as soon as I finish voicing my question, and he pulls me into his chest.

"Shit, Regina. I'm sorry. They've been transporting the girls to the tournament location one at a time in hopes of not raising any suspicion. You're one of the last on the docket, and I told them I'd take care of you and the other passion fruit by myself. Because this isn't exactly out of the norm, none of Burlone's men questioned my orders and left you both alone until I got here."

"I thought you said I wasn't going to the tournament?" I question.

"Plans changed."

"And what about Kingston?" My heart picks up its pace. "Is he going too?"

Giving me a single nod, Dex leans forward and brushes his lips against the shell of my ear. "Yes. But I promise that everything is going to be okay. We are all going to walk out of there. The plan is foolproof, but it won't work unless we're all there. We can't raise anyone's suspicion, understand?"

Peeking up at him, I release a shaky breath through my open mouth then give him a nod of my own, though I can't find my voice.

"Good. We're going to get you out of here. I promise. Are you ready for tonight?" he probes with a worried look.

With a dry laugh, I say, "Not particularly."

It's the moment I've been dreading since I woke up in Burlone's office with a pounding headache and missing clothes. The moment my brother always warned me could possibly happen if I wasn't careful. And instead of heeding his advice, I practically presented myself to the wolves with a little bow and a flashing neon sign that read, "*Hi! I'm Regina Romano. Come and get me.*"

I shake my head in an attempt to scatter my self-deprecation. It won't do me any good, anyway.

Dex squeezes me a little tighter. "Come here, Regina."

Burrowing into his embrace, I squeeze him just as tightly and try to hold back my tears. I've never been more terrified in my entire life, and I hate it.

"It's going to be okay." Gently, he rubs my back up and down, comforting me the best way he can.

"We really don't know that, Dex. If what you're saying is true, then my brother's coming tonight in an attempt to save me, but in reality, there's no guarantee either of us will walk out of there alive. And don't even get me started on you and the sacrifices you've already made for me." I squeeze my eyes shut as the familiar guilt swarms me from all sides. "I'm so sorry I've screwed up your whole world too. If anything happens to you, I'll—" I sound more like I'm choking than talking, my voice getting caught in my throat as it closes up. I feel like I've swallowed a handful of cotton balls, and they're making my mouth fumble through the words instead of speaking articulately. But the truth is, I can't imagine a world without Dex. The possibility is paralyzing.

The deep baritone rumbles through his chest and makes me cling to him closer. "Listen to me, Regina."

I stay silent.

"Listen, okay? I've already told you that your brother has a plan. Something that is fucking genius if we can pull it off, and honestly? If I didn't think it was a good one, I wouldn't consider sticking around to see how it would play out." He bends forward and brushes his mouth against my forehead before whispering against my skin, "It's going to be all right, Little Bird. I really, truly, think it will be. You just gotta be patient. And you need to trust us. It's going to work."

"And what if it doesn't?"

"Then I kill anyone who tries to touch you, and we escape through the back door where I have a Plan B set up. Just in case."

"Just in case?"

I look up to find him smiling softly. "Yeah. Just in case. I've got you, Little Bird. I promise."

With a sigh, I tighten my hold on his waist, squeezing him extra hard. "Alright, Dex. I trust you. What do you need from me?"

Releasing his hold, he tickles the oily strands of my hair that hang past my shoulders. "I need you to shower.

No offense, babe, but when was the last time you bathed?" His nose wrinkles dramatically, and I laugh, smacking him in the chest.

"Sorry about the hygiene issue, jackass. I've been a little tied up, if you know what I mean."

Throwing his head back, he joins in, shaking his head and laughing deeply. "Well, I think it's time we fix that. Don't you?"

My eyes light up at the prospect, making me almost forget the screwed up situation I'm blindly diving into. "Are you saying what I think you're saying?"

"And what do you think I'm saying?" he jests, tucking a strand of greasy hair behind my ear.

"You mean I get to shower? Please say yes." Lifting my hands up, I put my palms together and pretend to beg. "Seriously, I'd kill for a shower. I'll do anything. Please, please, please!"

"Anything?" he teases, quirking his brow.

I lift onto my tiptoes and give him a slow, sensual kiss with a hint of promise. Smirking mischievously, I add, "Anything."

Not even bothering to hide his groan, he grips my ass and tugs me closer. A soft gasp escapes me when I feel how hard he is. How ready. "If only, Little Bird. When this is all over, I'm making you pay up. But for now, let's get you that shower."

While I'm disappointed that I have to practice some patience, I can't stop the squeal that erupts at the opportunity to wash my hair.

"Yes! Do I get a razor too? Pleeease? I'm dying, Dex. For real...this is miserable."

"Yeah, Little Bird. You get a razor too. I even brought…." He eyes me wickedly, "Conditioner."

"Ooo…talk dirty to me."

"And a loofah."

"Bow-chica-bow-wow," I sing before throwing my arms around his shoulders and bringing him closer for another kiss, giggling when he nibbles my neck playfully in return. The glimpse I'm given of how we *could* be if we weren't in this messed-up situation is bittersweet, and I say a silent prayer that I'll get the chance to experience this side of him for more than a few stolen moments. I'd give anything for it.

When he backs away, I can see the sincerity in his irises, and I know that whatever he's about to say is coming from the heart, and it won't involve the innocent teasing from two minutes ago. I guess it's time to get back to reality, though I wish we could stay in the world of teasing, and giggling, and smiles, and carefree joy. I had forgotten what that was like before meeting Dex.

He makes me feel alive.

"Let's get through this, Regina. As soon as we do, I promise to treat you like the princess you are."

I want to cry at his declaration, but I hold back my tears, knowing they'll only put more pressure on him to fulfill his promise when I know we can't control what our future holds.

"As long as I have you, Dex, then I don't think I need anything else."

CHAPTER TWENTY-ONE

DEX

The drive to one of Burlone's estates a few miles away is short and quick. I can't take my eyes off the other passion fruit's busted up face, though. Sure, they tried to cover it up with some makeup and shit, but I can still see the marks.

"You okay?" I ask in a gruff voice with a glance in my rearview mirror. The windows are tinted to hide any onlookers from seeing them in the backseat of my black Audi, but I'm not sure it would matter much, anyway. We've already beaten them into submission. After all, that's one of Burlone's greatest selling points compared to his competitors. When they purchase fruit from him, they're purchasing docile fruit. He makes sure of it.

She doesn't answer me, confirming my suspicion that she's nothing but a walking corpse.

I watch Regina lean forward in her seat, attempting to make eye contact with her fellow prisoner, but she isn't successful. Still, her quiet voice murmurs, "Hi. Are you okay?"

Nothing.

From the back seat, Regina meets my gaze in the rearview mirror. Her concerned expression is highlighted by the passing headlights from the opposite side of the road. Helplessly, she gives me a soft shrug in her tight red dress as I turn onto a side road that leads to our destination.

I pull up to the back entrance of the estate then exit the car. After slipping the key into my front pocket, I open the back door to let the girls slide out. The wind blows a bit of Regina's hair away from her face as her heel-clad feet touch the ground. She looks stunning. A stylist had curled her long hair after she had a chance to shower, but she left it cascading down Regina's back. It's gorgeous. She also added some makeup to her clear complexion. It's the first time I've seen her all dolled up, and I hate that she'll be paraded around tonight like a prized pony, but it doesn't change the fact that she's hot as hell.

Licking her plump lips, she inspects the giant house that is hosting the tournament as we both wait for the other girl to get out of the back seat.

When she doesn't, I release a sigh and bend forward, popping my head through the doorway.

"Come on, darlin'. We need to get inside."

She doesn't move a muscle.

"Please?" I try again; the pleading feels foreign on my tongue. I'm not used to asking for favors, but it seems I've been doing it a lot since Regina fell into my lap.

The sound of heavy boots crunching the gravel along the side of the house grabs my attention.

"What are you doing out here?" My voice is hard and cold as I address the culprit.

"You're late. All the other girls are in their places at the table. Their buyers are wondering where they are." He motions to Regina and the other passion fruit who still hasn't budged.

"We're coming."

With a smirk, Sei offers, "Want me to take it from here?"

"I've got it. Thanks."

"Apparently, you don't because one of them is having a little trouble getting out of the car, isn't she?"

"I said, I've got it," I grit out.

"I'm sure you do. If we had all day, I'd let you prove it. Unfortunately, Burlone is getting impatient, and you know what that means. Now, would you like me to escort the one who's being a good piece of fruit, or would you like me to handle the difficult one?"

"I'll go," Regina interjects, her eyes the size of saucers as she puts herself in such a precarious position.

My jaw tightens. "You'll stay with me."

Laughing, Sei steps closer. "I knew you'd chosen favorites."

"It's fine," Regina states, ignoring Sei. "Sei will just... escort me upstairs. Right, Sei?"

His amusement is clear as Sei registers Regina's suggestion that borders an order. "Exactly. I'll just...escort her upstairs," he offers, repeating her exact words.

My gut tightens, but Regina doesn't wait to hear my response. She turns on her heel and starts marching toward the entrance. With a grin, Sei watches her ass sway back and forth for a few seconds before mentioning, "She's a ripe piece of fruit, isn't she? Tell me, how does she taste?"

A low growl rumbles up my throat, but he raises his hand. "Don't worry. I'm not stupid enough to touch her until Burlone's plan comes to a head. Besides, my hands have been plenty full with the peach in the back of your car." Leaning closer to me, he drops his voice low. "Want to know a secret?"

"What's that?"

"He's even going to let me keep her." His mouth stretches wide, reminding me of a little kid on Christmas who was gifted the perfect present.

"Who?" I ask, confused.

Cocking his head toward my car, his eyes practically sparkle. "Don't forget to put her collar on nice and tight. See you inside." Then he rushes after Regina, leaving me alone with a girl whose fate is worse than death.

CHAPTER TWENTY-TWO

REGINA

I can feel him stalking closer as I walk up the steps to the back entrance. It takes everything inside of me to keep my spine straight instead of cowering away from him. Hands shaking, I reach for the door handle and twist.

I didn't want to leave Dex's side. It almost killed me. But I could tell that the other girl needed him more than I did in that moment, and I wasn't about to leave her alone with Sei. Not when she was already so broken.

A hand pushes me from behind, and I fall to my knees.

Gasping in pain, I look over my shoulder to see an amused Sei staring down at me. "So this is what you look like on your knees," he notes. His eyes darken at the prospect. "Interesting."

"Don't we have somewhere we need to be?" I return, barely keeping the trembling from my voice.

His hand comes out of nowhere, smacking me across the face. My head swings to the side as a sharp ache explodes across my cheekbone. My mouth opens wide in pain, but I don't say anything in an attempt to keep him from snapping a second time.

"Good girl," he praises. "You're learning."

Squeezing my eyes shut, I clutch at my bruised cheek that's tender as hell.

"Get up and put your hands out. We have some special jewelry for you this evening."

I do as I'm told and watch him cuff my wrists together before placing another piece of metal around my neck. It's so tight, I feel like I'm suffocating. When I look into his dark, beady eyes, I realize that's exactly what he's hoping for.

And I hate him even more for it.

"Beautiful," he mutters under his breath, dragging his finger against the column of my throat while admiring his handiwork. The sound of the backdoor squeaking grabs his attention, and I swallow thickly. When my gaze connects with Dex's, I want to cry and run into his strong arms, but I try to stay strong.

"You touched her," Dex growls, assessing my bruised cheek.

"I had to remind her of her place. Seems she's forgotten while under your supervision."

Dex takes a step forward when Burlone walks in and interrupts, "What the hell is taking you both so long? Dex, get the fruit upstairs. Now. Sei, we're still waiting on our guest of honor. Greet them at the door and make sure he knows our standard protocol. Understand?"

I watch both men nod, though Dex's is much more jerky than Sei's.

Satisfied, Burlone exits the room just as quickly as he'd entered. There's so much tension remaining from his absence that I'm afraid I'll drown in it.

"Sure you don't need any more help?" Sei offers condescendingly.

Ignoring him, Dex quips, "Better run along, Sei. Wouldn't want to keep the guest of honor waiting."

Sei gives him a final glare then disappears through a second doorway that I assume leads to the entrance. Once he's gone, Dex's hand gently caresses my throbbing cheek.

"You okay?"

I nod. "I'll be fine once this is over."

Dropping his hand from my face, he gives me a somber look then cuffs the second girl before guiding us upstairs through a back stairwell. The opulence in the open room is staggering, but I'm too distracted by the filth in the space camouflaged in black tuxedos and silk ties to appreciate it fully.

Jaw tight, Dex tugs on the cuffs and leads me to an old man with salt and pepper hair before urging me to place my hand on his shoulder. My brows furrow in confusion.

"Look around, Little Bird," he mutters under his breath. "Follow their lead. Blend in. And do anything they ask you to do without question. If you don't, there'll be consequences."

It's the last line that makes me pause until I remember there are witnesses here, and the cool, indifferent Dex is back with a vengeance.

Digging my teeth into my lower lip, I nod. "Yes, sir."

"Good girl."

Then he's gone, and I'm left standing around a poker

table like a little piece of fruit while the despicable men leer at me from all sides.

And I can't wait to watch them all burn.

CHAPTER TWENTY-THREE

DEX

*T*aking a deep breath, I roll my shoulders and release the pent-up oxygen through my mouth. It about killed me to leave Regina all by herself in a room full of human traffickers, but I needed to cover all my bases, which includes a certain nemesis who has no idea what's coming to him.

When I see Sei round the corner from the front door with a cigarette hanging from his mouth, I raise my arm and motion him to come closer. I assume he's just finished greeting Kingston and Ace, which means it's time.

"Hey, what's up?" he asks, lifting his chin while remaining completely oblivious to the fact that his world is about to get rocked. It's always amazed me that he can be so conniving, yet so blind at the same time. He knows that I'm likely still pissed about him touching Regina, but he also thinks he's protected. Hell, he thinks he's a god. That he's untouchable. He's in for a rude awakening.

"There's been a change of plans," I explain, keeping my voice even.

"And what's that?"

Taking another casual step closer while confirming that we're very much alone in the empty hallway, I keep my hand at my side and flick off the lid on the syringe that's filled with a homemade concoction meant to bring down a gorilla.

Sei notices the minor movement, and his brows pull together in confusion.

"What's going on?"

Clearing my throat, I explain, "I grew a conscience."

Sei's eyes widen in shock as I lift my arm to strike, but he dodges my move at the last instant, and the syringe only finds air. Turning around, I'm sucker-punched in the kidney, followed by a swift kick to my arm that makes me lose my grip on the needle. The syringe flies through the air before skidding across the ground.

I snap my attention back to Sei, making sure to keep my front to him as we slowly start to circle each other. The familiarity reminds me of all our times in the ring during our hours off before Regina came into my care and consumed me completely.

My mouth quirks up on one side. "Scared, Sei?"

Growling, he lunges forward. I counter the move by stepping to the side, landing a swift uppercut he never sees coming. When my fist connects with his jaw, his head swings to the side followed by a spray of crimson saliva, and shit, it feels good. Sei shakes off my punch then ducks low, ramming his shoulder into my stomach.

With a huff, I stumble a few steps before wrapping my arm around his neck and shoving my knee into his ribcage. Floundering, Sei lets me out of his hold, bends down, and reaches for the knife he keeps strapped to his ankle. But I know him too well. Reading his intentions, I kick him in the face, and he drops to the ground like a bag of bricks.

"You can't fight this, Sei. Burlone's time is up. He needs to be dethroned from his screwed-up empire, and you need to be put down too."

Spitting a mouth full of blood, Sei slowly gets to his knees. "Go to hell, Dex. What makes you think you can take down Burlone?"

I shrug off his question and reach for his knife that had skidded across the marble flooring before squatting low and getting in Sei's face. "There's a new king in town. One that has morals I can align with."

Scoffing, Sei mutters, "Of course, you did. You've always been a little bitch with family issues, Dex. I guess I shouldn't be surprised you crumbled under Burlone's reign and decided to run to brother dearest for help. But what's that saying? Once a traitor, always a traitor?"

I clench my jaw. "Shut the hell up, Sei."

"Make me," he growls, completely disregarding the knife that hovers a few inches from his face.

With a shake of my head and a flick of my wrist, I slice a three-inch gash from his diamond tattoo below his eye down to his jaw.

As he grabs his cheek in agony, I tsk, "Don't test me, Sei. I might have a soft spot for innocent women, but I'm not afraid to remove every inch of skin from your body."

Slowly, Sei drops his hand from his cheek and peers up at me with so much hate, I'm surprised I'm still standing. "You gonna kill me, Dex? We might not be blood, but we were raised together. You'd throw that away?"

"In a heartbeat," I laugh. "Now get up, and get in the

closet, and don't try anything, or I'll make that pretty little gash on your face look like a paper cut."

For once in his life, Sei listens and pushes himself up from the ground with his hands raised in the air. Apparently, he does have a sense of self-preservation. I watch as the blood drips down his cheek and off his chin in rivulets. Tilting my head to a small coat closet, Sei turns on his heel and gives me his back before plopping into the chair I'd placed there earlier. I take a moment to pick up the unused syringe then follow him inside.

"You gonna cuff me or kill me?" he asks, though he looks indifferent either way.

With a shrug, I offer, "Maybe both," before lunging forward and driving the needle into his neck, plunging the concoction into his veins. I watch in fascination as his eyes roll back, and his head lolls forward.

Cautiously, I make sure he's really out then cuff him to the chair.

"Goodbye, Sei. Hope you enjoy prison."

CHAPTER TWENTY-FOUR

REGINA

*O*nce Dex disappears, I'm left with a growing sense of unease as I listen to the men surrounding the poker table. One mentions a delayed import that is causing him issues with the Mexican cartel. I assume he means drugs. Another brings up basketball and his money laundering business that he hopes will be more successful this year. I almost roll my eyes, growing more bored by the second when movement by the entrance grabs my attention.

With a girl on his arm, my brother appears over the threshold, and it takes me a second to recognize his guest for the evening.

My jaw drops.

What the hell is she doing here? I think to myself, my breathing growing more and more shallow by the second. My gaze shoots to my brother, but he's too busy assessing the entire room to notice me. I guess I shouldn't be that surprised. He's here for one reason, and even his little sister won't distract him from finding success.

"Gentlemen, I'm glad you could all make it," Burlone starts, distracting me from Ace's terrified expression. My throat tightens, but I try to concentrate on what he's saying. "Now, as you all know, the rule is a simple winner-takes-all format. However, while I've been gracious enough to prepare your women for you, none of you have compensated me for my efforts in acquiring them. Instead, you requested to pay in person this evening before the official tournament started. As you all know, this is highly irregular, but I've been generous enough to comply. Well, gentlemen, the time has arrived. Now, if you will...." His voice trails off as he motions to the table, silently asking the slimy assholes willing to sell and buy women sitting around the table to pay up.

No one moves a muscle.

With my heart racing, I watch my brother while assuming this was his doing. He doesn't move an inch. And neither does anyone else.

Clearing his throat, Burlone tries again. "I'm sorry, were those instructions confusing? I mean, I know there's an open bar and all but—" He chuckles awkwardly at his pathetic joke while the rest of the room stays motionless.

"You're awfully insistent we pay up," the man to my left mutters under his breath.

With his salt and pepper hair slicked back, the stranger is busy fiddling with his hands as his gaze springs around the room in search of backup before landing firmly on Kingston, who looks like a freaking statue. Clearly, my brother is biding his time. I just don't know what he's waiting for.

Speak up, Kingston! I want to shout, but I keep my

mouth shut tight. And where the hell is Dex? I peek over my shoulder but don't find him.

"Excuse me?" Burlone scoffs. "Dex, escort Mr. Carbonne from the premises." At the mention of Dex, I continue my search with renewed fervor while trying to look inconspicuous. Burlone adds, "It seems he's misunderstood the dynamic of our relationship. But don't worry, I'm sure we can find a way to rectify that as quickly as possible with a little persuasion."

Mr. Carbonne, however, gulps loudly before tugging on the collar of his button-up as if it's choking him. I want to laugh at the irony since the girl behind him is literally wearing a collar too, just like the rest of us women in the room.

From the shadows, my savior appears with a cocky smirk that makes me want to melt. Casually, he rests a handgun at his side. "Apologies, Mr. Allegretti. But I'm afraid I can't do that."

"Excuse me?" Burlone turns in his seat with a glare, searching for Dex around the perimeter of the room. When he finds him, his gaze narrows.

"What the hell are you doing?" Burlone grits out.

"Nothing." Dex shrugs. "Just making sure to keep everything in check, which means Mr. Carbonne gets to stay here for a bit longer."

"Have you forgotten your place, Dex?"

"No, I've found it," he returns, his eyes finding Kingston's for a split second before returning to Burlone. But it's long enough for Burlone to start piecing things together. His mouth opens in disbelief.

"Sei!" Burlone shouts. His neck snaps to the front of the room as he searches for his other loyal soldier, and I find myself doing the same thing, but he's nowhere to be found.

"I'm afraid Sei's not available at the moment," Dex adds conversationally. "And neither are the rest of your men."

"What the fuck did you do?"

"Just taking out the trash, Burlone. And those that didn't need my assistance in disappearing were generously compensated. I'm sure you understand," Dex explains. Motioning to Kingston, he adds, "Boss, I think now would be a great time to step in."

Kingston chuckles darkly, gaining the attention of everyone in the room as the spotlight shifts from one man to another. I don't miss the way Dex calls him boss, and I'm positive everyone else here heard it loud and clear too.

"I dunno, Dex. I think this is rather entertaining, don't you?" Kingston finally voices. Not a single person utters a word. They're all too engrossed in the scene unveiling around them. Just like me.

"What the fuck is going on?" Burlone bellows angrily. He's sweating like a sinner in church, and it takes everything inside of me to keep my expression blank when I want to grin at his discomfort.

Go to hell, bastard.

"Alright, alright. I'll step in," my brother interrupts, not bothering to contain his amusement. He's always been a cocky sonofabitch. I always thought I hated that about him, but right now, I want to cheer him on with a set of pom-poms and a catchy tune that gets the crowd as invested as I am.

"Dex came to me recently. Can you believe that, Burlone?" Kingston asks though he's addressing the whole room. Hell, he's commanding it. "Your own right-hand man? I thought it was a little out of character too, but Dex felt the need to voice a suspicion he had about his dear old boss. Secret meetings. Intentionally botched drop-offs. I found it fascinating, so I decided to do a little research of my own. What I found was...*interesting,* to say the least."

Burlone shakes his head in disbelief. "What the hell are you talking about, King?"

Yeah, what the hell are you talking about? I want to ask. My eyes find Dex's. He gives me a subtle wink, silently reminding me that everything is going to be okay before turning his attention back to Burlone.

"I'm talking about your association with the FBI and your plan to incriminate everyone at this table tonight as soon as they handed over their money for the beautiful women you've *found.*" The way King says the word *found* is enough to insinuate the opposite.

Burlone sputters, "What the hell does that mean?"

"Dex," King calls while ignoring Burlone completely.

Gun at his side, Dex steps out of the shadows. "Yeah, Boss?"

"Were the women in this room handled differently than usual?"

"Yeah."

"Care to expand?" My brother prods with a dry laugh.

Dex joins in before explaining, "The men were explicitly told *not* to touch them. In fact, Burlone brought me in and ordered me to keep them from being spoiled before they were officially purchased, which he's never done before. If we're being honest, he's usually one of the first to break them in."

The men around the room all laugh, and my brother

joins in, pretending to be one of them when I know for a fact that he finds the situation just as despicable as Dex does.

"And why do you think they were being protected?" Kingston probes.

"Because he didn't want any incriminating evidence on the Allegretti family. Only his associates."

"And why is that?"

"Because he cut a deal with the Feds," Dex finishes, matter-of-factly.

Burlone's outrage is palpable as he shoves his chair away from the table a few inches but stays seated in the process. "That's bullshit, and you know it. Gentlemen, why would I talk to the Feds? It's not logical."

"It is if they've got incriminating evidence against you like your former soldier just stated," Mr. Carbonne pipes in while crossing his arms over his large, round chest. "It makes sense for you to work out a deal with the Feds to help them gather evidence against your associates instead of arresting you. Selfish, Burlone. But smart. *If* you hadn't been caught."

Burlone rolls his eyes. "That's the most ludicrous thing I've ever heard. What kind of evidence do you have? You can't honestly believe the high and mighty Romano family over one of your own?"

Another man interrupts next to Kingston. He's got to be almost sixty years old and looks like an old bulldog, his jowls hanging off his face. "Interestingly, I would normally agree with you, Burlone. But then I heard from one of my associates who informed me of a little incident a few weeks ago. One where you had set up a drop-off on Kingston's turf but didn't show up with the women.

However, the Feds *did* know where you were meeting and were there to greet him. The only reason my associate didn't get caught was because the Romano family stepped in and screwed up your plans. I assume that's why you personally named Kingston Romano in the email invitation to this tournament. To incriminate him when we all know he's never been one to dabble in the skin trade. You wanted to use the email against him in a court of law."

This was the night Kingston warned me to stay home. It was the night I snuck out to meet Ace at Dottie's. It was the night I was kidnapped.

"This is all hearsay. There's no proof," Burlone defends, but I can feel the tide turning in our favor. I think everyone can.

"And if there was proof?" Kingston interrupts the conversation, taking control of the room with a simple question.

Do they have proof? What kind of proof? What the hell is going on?

Burlone's face gets splotchy and red. His mouth opens and closes like a fish out of water, playing right into Kingston's hands. "I-it's not possible."

"I'm going to have to respectfully disagree, my friend."

CHAPTER TWENTY-FIVE

DEX

*W*ith a snap of Kingston's fingers, I stalk closer and put my gun to Burlone's head, ensuring he doesn't move. Damn, it feels good. Lifting his hand, Kingston covers his girlfriend's as it rests on his shoulder. The touch is intimate, proving his feelings for her. When Burlone sees it, he practically vibrates with anger while I vibrate with guilt for beating the shit out of her two weeks ago.

"Hey, Wild Card," Kingston murmurs. "Can you excuse me for a minute?"

She smiles nervously, then takes a slow step back and lets him scoot out of his chair. Rounding the table, Kingston rests his hip against the black felt top of the poker table and towers over Burlone. Every single person watches his movements with rapt attention, and if Kingston were anyone else, I'm certain he'd crumble from the pressure.

"Do you know what we do to traitors, Burlone?"

"I'm not a fucking traitor, Kingston," Burlone spits. I

press the barrel of the gun harder into his temple to remind him of his place.

"Well, let's see what our fellow associates have to say then, shall we?" Kingston looks around the table. "Gentlemen? If you think this man deserves to die a slow and painful death, raise your hand. If you don't, then I'll let him go, you'll pay for your women, and we'll play the tournament as if this never happened."

I don't move a muscle as I look around the room to see if the sorry sacks of shit have bought our lie. Slowly, one after another, hands are raised into the air.

All except one.

Fucking Russo. I shouldn't be surprised. Out of everyone here, he's always had the closest relationship with Burlone. They've never had a problem seeing eye to eye on things, and if anyone were ever to replace Burlone, it'd be him.

"There a problem, Mr. Russo?" Kingston asks with a bored expression.

"I've seen your evidence," he begins. "I've seen the official FBI letterhead with his picture on it. But I know Burlone, and I'm having a hard time believing what you've shown me. I think you'll need to give me a bit more proof before I can condemn someone I once considered a friend to a traitorous death."

I open my mouth to interject when a feminine voice distracts me.

"Burlone?"

All heads swivel in the same direction where the other passion fruit, Sei's particular favorite, squares her shoulders. "Do you know what the FBI does to traitors?"

A ghost of a smile graces my lips before I cover it with indifference as the room goes deathly silent.

Good girl, I think to myself. *Throw him to the wolves. Watch him burn for what he did to you. What he did to all of you.*

Glaring at Burlone, she continues, "We toss them back to their own kind, letting them fend for themselves."

Burlone shifts in his seat before gritting out, "What the fuck are you talking about, bitch? Shut your filthy mouth before I make you."

"Shhh," she tsks as if she were talking to a toddler. The lifeless girl from the car has been replaced with a confident woman who oozes disgust from every pore on her porcelain complexion. My chest swells with pride.

"I'm an undercover agent for the Federal Bureau of Investigation, and we had a deal. As soon as you found a buyer for me, and the transaction went through, we'd storm the castle, throw your friends in jail, and you'd be off the hook. However, there was one condition I had. Do you remember what it was?"

Burlone opens his mouth to answer, but I slam the butt of my handgun into the back of his head, making his neck snap forward and his chin drop to his chest. In a daze, he shakes his head, so the girl answers for him.

"You guaranteed my protection. You told me I wouldn't be touched. But I was...countless times. And now, your associates know the truth. You're a traitor, and I hope they make you pay for it slowly and in the most painful way possible."

Burlone sputters, "I-if you were an FBI agent, why would you out yourself in a room full of mafia bosses?"

She shrugs. "I'm dead, anyway. Might as well take one

asshole who's a liar down with me for what he did. Mr. Russo, you said you wanted proof. Now, you have it. He's a traitor who was plotting against all of you with my team to save his own skin. If I weren't guaranteed to be dead by the end of this conversation, I'd give you physical evidence as a nice little cherry on top. But for now, you'll have to take my word for it."

The room floods with questions from everyone, buzzing at a pitch that is almost unrecognizable until Mr. Russo straightens his tie then turns to Kingston. "And now, you have my vote. Gut the poor bastard. And she's right. Make it slow. Make it hurt. Make him pay for being a rat."

"With pleasure." Kingston smiles. "Unfortunately, my utility bag is at home, and we don't know how long we have until the Feds storm the castle, as the undercover agent so eloquently stated, so I think we'll be going. Dex?"

"Yeah?" I answer.

"I'm going to need you to escort *her* to my car too." He tilts his head toward the girl who saved the day. The order seems to put the rest of the room at ease with the promise of her demise. In reality, he won't be touching a hair on her head. Not after everything she just did for us. Without her, Mr. Russo wouldn't have been swayed, and we'd all be dead.

"Done." Slamming the gun against Burlone's head with more force than the previous time, his body slumps in his chair. Satisfied he won't be waking up anytime soon, I reach into my suit pocket and pull out a set of zip ties before placing them around Burlone's slackened wrists and ankles. I turn to the pseudo-FBI girl, wishing I'd bothered to ask her name before now, and try to keep up the ruse by asking, "Do you want to do this the easy way or the hard way?"

With tears in her eyes, she whispers, "I'm done fighting. It never did me much good, anyway."

Nodding, I toss an unconscious Burlone over my shoulder, then reach for her handcuffs and pull her toward the back entrance that leads to my car. I'll be back for Regina in a second.

The sound of Mr. Carbonne's voice is cut off when the heavy door closes with a thud.

CHAPTER TWENTY-SIX

DEX

*T*he car is tense as we drive to Kingston's estate. Regina is sitting in the front seat, looking beautiful yet exhausted at the same time. My jaw tightens as I examine the blossoming bruise on her face that Sei gifted her with while I was helping the other passion fruit out of the car earlier this evening.

Gently, I run my finger across it another time, and she looks over at me. "It doesn't hurt, Dex. I promise. Stop beating yourself up about it. We made it out of there, and that's all that matters."

Regina must sense my unease because she puts her hand on top of mine before lacing our fingers and resting them in her lap. "Seriously, Dex. I'm fine. We can play *doctor* later, and you can bring me back to health, okay?" She winks for good measure, fizzling out a bit of the guilt rolling in my stomach.

"Deal."

As I accelerate, Burlone's body rolls around in the trunk, making me smile until I remember to check my rearview mirror. The girl I was supposed to protect--but failed to do so--sits in the back by herself with her arms wrapped around her chest, staring blankly out the window. Again.

With an unsure voice, Regina turns in her seat and asks, "Hey. Are you okay?"

I'm not surprised when the girl doesn't answer.

"I'm Regina. I was taken two weeks ago. Just like you. What's your name?"

Not bothering to give us her full attention, the girl whispers, "Quenna. You can call me Q."

"Can I ask you something, Q?" Regina probes.

"Sure."

"Do you really work for the FBI?"

I watch as her tongue darts out from between her lips, and she looks over at me through the rearview mirror. "Will you think I'm lying if I say no?"

She isn't asking Regina. She's asking me. And I already know the answer. There's no way in hell she's working for the Feds. Or at least...I don't think so. Regardless, it doesn't matter. She saved us back there, and I won't forget it.

"No, Q. I won't think you're lying," I reply, turning my attention back to the winding road as we make our way to Kingston's estate.

"Then I guess you have your answer."

"But why lie to those men?" I prod. I'm happy she did it, but I can't help but search for an explanation when I have so many questions.

"Because I was going to die, anyway. Might as well make Burlone join me, right?"

Next to me, Regina laughs. "Amen, Q. Maybe my

brother will let us get in a few good swings with a baseball bat before he finishes Burlone off. What do you say to that?"

And for the first time since I've met her, I see Q smile. "I think that sounds fan-freaking-tastic."

* * *

As we pull up to the house, Ace rushes toward us and swings the passenger door open on my car before practically tackling Regina with hugs.

"G! I've missed you so much! I can't believe you're Kingston's sister! I had no idea. Neither of us did. Your brother thought it was hilarious, by the way. Are you okay? I couldn't find you. I've been freaking out. I'm so glad you're here." The words keep tumbling out of her as she squeezes the shit out of my Little Bird.

With a soft laugh, Regina returns her embrace. "I'll be okay, Ace. And I'm glad my brother doesn't want to shoot me for putting all of you through the wringer."

"You'll be fine. Promise. Come on." Ace grabs her hand and starts to lead her into the house when Regina stops her.

"I'll be right there. Do you think you could take Q in for me?"

Ace tilts her head before registering Queena in the back.

"Oh. Hi. I'm Ace. And you're Q?"

Q stares blankly out the window, not bothering to respond. She does that a lot.

Tossing a wide-eyed look of helplessness our way, Ace hesitantly opens the back door and offers her hand.

"Come on, Q. Let's get you inside and out of those cuffs and dress."

Apparently, the promise of freedom is enough to get Q moving. She slides out of the car and follows Ace inside, leaving me alone with my girl.

"Alright, babe, let's get you out of these cuffs." I reach for the keys in my pocket that I'd swiped from Sei and unlatch the locks with ease as Regina watches my every movement. Once she's free, we head toward the front door in silence, and I can tell something is bothering her.

"Guess it's time to face my brother, huh?" Regina states sadly.

I stop her from entering the house and turn her around until we're chest to chest. "What's wrong, Little Bird?"

"I don't know how much you know about me," she hedges. "But I was pretty much bred to be a bargaining chip with another family. Combining bloodlines and all that." She waves her hand in the air while a light sheen of tears gathers in her eyes.

"I may have heard that," I confirm, watching her closely.

"I've been a brat to Kingston my entire life. Between my disappearance, and my future, I'm a little freaked out to talk to him. Especially when I tell him what I want." Looking up at me, she whispers, "I'm terrified he'll say no."

"And what do you want, Little Bird?"

Her heels are busy kicking a few pebbles across the pavement before she peeks up at me. "What do you think I want?"

I shake my head. "That's not what I asked. You're

allowed to have your own opinions. Your own wants. Your own needs."

With a gulp, she probes, "There's only one thing I want and need, Dex. And after the hell I've been through, I'm pretty sure you can guess what it is. I think the real question is, do you want it too?"

"I put my life on the line for you, Little Bird. You're my oxygen, remember? But you're right. Your brother holds all the cards right now and hiding out here isn't going to give us our answer. We need to be brave. Together. We've already been through more than anyone should ever have to endure. I think we can make it past your brother's verdict too."

Her hand is trembling as she lifts it and touches the side of my face, piercing me with her hypnotic eyes. "I think I'm in love with you, Dex. No matter what my brother says in there, that's not going to change, okay? I just…I need you to know that."

Bending closer, I brush my lips against hers then whisper, "Have a little faith, Regina. It's going to work out."

"You don't know how awful I was to him. How much harder I made his life just because I was grieving and thought he didn't care—"

"Regina. Give your brother a little more credit. It's going to be fine," I reiterate.

"How can you be so sure?"

With a confident smirk, I razz, "'Cause he owes me."

My sarcasm is enough to break her somber attitude, and she responds by smacking me in the chest.

"I guess we'll just have to wait and see." Then, she heads to the front door while I trail behind, enjoying the view of her round ass in a tight red dress.

"Like what you see?" she calls over her shoulder.

"Maybe," I throw back at her before rushing up the steps and grabbing her hand. Together, we walk through the expansive foyer and toward Kingston's office. Because I know that with her by my side, we can get through anything.

CHAPTER TWENTY-SEVEN

DIECE

I can't take my eyes off the girl who's clinging to Ace's hand like it's a lifeline. Soft blonde hair, sexy black dress, perfectly polished complexion. There are remnants of discolored skin on her upper arm along with what looks like the shadow of a bruise below her right eye, but I can't be sure unless I get a closer look.

I've been watching her for the past five minutes while the room is blanketed in silence as we all wait for Dex and Regina to join us. As the time ticks by, I've decided I could do it for an eternity, and it still wouldn't be enough. The way she lets her hair hang down, covering the side of her face, pretending it's a barrier between her and the outside world. The way her hands are trembling, but she tries to cover it up by clenching them into tight little fists. The way her eyes keep darting to mine before staring down at the hardwood floor like it's the most fascinating thing on the planet.

Everything. Everything about her is mesmerizing. As if

she's a puzzle piece I can't quite place. Which is ironic because that's *exactly* what she is.

How the hell we ended up with her in Kingston's house is beyond me, and I'm anxious to be filled in. I assume she's Ace's missing friend, Gigi, but I don't know why she's down here waiting to speak with King and the rest of the family when, if she were simply Ace's friend, she'd already be tucked away in the guest room to recover from her ordeal. Or at least, that's what I would guess, anyway.

From the corner of my eye, a flash of movement demands my attention. I'm on my feet and rushing toward Regina before she even steps into the room. Throwing my arms around her, I lift her up and give her a heavy hug that leaves her gasping for air.

She slaps my back and squeaks, "Let me go, you big oaf!"

With a laugh, I release her, and I'm joined by Stefan and Lou, who both pull her into their own embraces too.

"How are you doing, Regina? King has a doctor on call in case you need it."

She waves me off. "I'm fine, D. Promise. Your brother took good care of me."

The casualness in which she brought him up is staggering, making me feel like I got sucker-punched. We still haven't really addressed our familial ties other than a few offhand comments in the car that first day we met. I'm not sure if I'm ready to get into it in a room full of spectators.

With a simple nod directed at him, I say, "Hey. How'd it go?"

"Good. Burlone's still in the trunk. Where do you want

me to put him?" Dex asks, shifting his weight uncomfortably.

"We have a shed out back," I offer. "But, let's catch up with King first."

"Speaking of which, way to steal my thunder, D. She's my sister, remember?" King argues, marching toward Regina and tugging her close.

"I'm so sorry," Regina begins with a hushed apology. Sensing their need for privacy, I take a step back and find the mysterious blonde staring at me with restrained curiosity and a bit of hatred too. I haven't done a damn thing to her, but the animosity is palpable. When our gazes connect, hers snaps down to her hands as they fumble with the tight black material of her dress.

Clearing my throat, I pull my attention up to the ceiling before a sniffle from Regina commands my focus again. Hastily, she wipes away a few tears from her face then leans into Dex's side. Without a word, he wraps his arm around her waist and kisses the top of her head. I don't miss the display of affection, and neither does Kingston. But he doesn't comment on it. Not yet.

"Well, since we're all here and we've had our little reunion," Kingston begins, "I figured it'd be best to get everyone caught up. Dex, where's Burlone?"

"Still in the trunk. D said he'd show me the shed in a few," Dex answers.

Stefan interrupts, "I'll do it. Just give me your keys."

After digging into his pockets, Dex tosses them through the air, and Stefan catches them before disappearing out the door. Seconds later, Dex throws another key at Ace and drops his chin to her friend's cuffs. While Ace unlocks them, Kingston gets to the next order of business. And I'm just as anxious as everyone else in the room to see what he has to say on the matter.

"Good. As far as your loyalty goes, you've earned your spot in the Romano family. I'll make an announcement tomorrow. You're blood, Dex. Through and through."

CHAPTER TWENTY-EIGHT

DEX

Kingston's declaration nearly brings me to my knees, but I keep my balance steady and attempt to maintain a semblance of control. I never thought I'd hear those words. I'm an outcast. I've always been an outcast. But it seems redemption just might be in order. Maybe my soul isn't lost after all.

My gaze shoots to Diece a few feet away before dropping to Regina.

"And what about her?" The question is clear in my voice. The room goes silent as we all wait for the rest of Kingston's verdict. One that will make or break me.

"Let me ask you something, Dex," Kingston says carefully, lifting his chin to my Little Bird. "Do you know who she is?"

With my heart pounding in my chest, I answer, "Of course."

"Tell me."

Cocking my head, I give him the most watered-down response possible. "She's Regina Romano."

"And who is Regina Romano?"

I open my mouth to reply, but he cuts me off. "She's the princess of the Romano family. She's the daughter of Gabriel and Emilia Romano and sister to Kingston Romano, the head of the Romano family. Now let me ask you this. Who. Are. You?" With three simple words, I know I have my answer. And I want to kill him for it.

My jaw flexes until I'm sure I'll crack a molar, but I know I'm on thin ice right now. I can feel it in my bones. If I mess up this conversation, it'll be the end of everything.

"Answer the question," Kingston pushes. His eyes are laser-focused as he waits to see who I truly serve. Whether it's him or his sister. And it's in this moment that I realize if I ever want to call his sister mine, then I need to earn his trust first. I just hope it doesn't gut Regina the same way it guts me.

"Dex," I grit out.

"Just Dex?"

"Yes."

Tapping his chin, Kingston leans forward. "And why is that?"

"Because my father didn't claim me," I growl, unable to hide my frustration at the asshole in front of me, who is now my fucking boss.

"No. He didn't. You're nothing but a bastard. Regina Romano is so far out of your league that you'd be lucky to clean the shit off her shoes."

He's not wrong. I know this. He knows this. Pretty sure anyone who has ever laid eyes on Regina would know this. But it doesn't stop him from twisting the knife in my chest, now does it?

"Kingston, please—" Regina interrupts, her voice cracking as she attempts to beg for her happiness. Kingston cuts her off with a cold, hard look.

I'm not surprised in the least.

"Regina, I know you have feelings for him, but have you ever considered the possibility that those feelings are based off who you perceived him to be when you didn't have anyone else? You barely know him."

Shiiit.

He's right. What if her feelings for me aren't real? What if they've been woven together out of desperation and self-preservation?

"It doesn't matter, King. I know that I—"

"Stop!" he shouts, cutting her off.

My entire body tenses, every muscle pulling tight, ready to be released on my enemy as the overwhelming need to protect Regina pulses through me.

Yell at her again, and I kill you, I silently challenge him, but I keep my mouth shut. It doesn't matter if he's my new boss or that he's her brother. It doesn't matter if her feelings for me are real or if they've been fabricated. She's been through enough over the past two weeks and deserves a little respect. And if he doesn't start giving it to her, I'm going to put a bullet in his skull.

Regina's quivering lips pull into a thin line, but she doesn't respond.

"Regina, you're dismissed," Kingston orders. "Go to your room and wash up. Dex, if you'd still like a place here as a soldier, I'll give it to you. You've earned it. However, if you plan to pursue my sister, I'll tell you right now that you'll be gutted for it. Understand?"

Regina storms off without waiting for my response,

and I'm glad she doesn't have to witness me bending for her brother. I just pray that by the time this is all over, she'll understand why.

"Kingston—" Ace interrupts in an attempt to soothe him. He gives her a pointed look that dares her to continue. She doesn't finish her sentence.

"Not now, Ace. I'm not going to change my mind, but if you'd like to discuss it further, we'll discuss it in private. Understand?"

She nods.

"Good. Now, next order of business. You." He points to Q, who's still busy clutching Ace's hand like it's a lifeline. "What's your name?"

Like always, she doesn't bother to answer him, so Ace does it for her. "Her name is Q."

"I thought her name was Gigi?" Diece interjects, looking confused as hell.

Rolling her eyes, Ace clarifies, "Regina is my friend who went missing. She's my Gigi. We met at Dottie's one night and bonded over coffee and breakfast food. Q is just an innocent bystander who got caught in Burlone's crosshairs and ended up saving the day."

Gaze narrowing in suspicion, Kingston addresses Q. "Speaking of which, what the hell happened in that room, and why did you do it?"

Q keeps up her corpse-like behavior, staring blankly in front of her until Ace nudges her softly with her shoulder.

Clearing her throat, Q answers, "You needed my help, and I was dead, anyway."

"But why help me?"

With a quick look at Ace, Q mutters, "I saw her walk in

with you. I saw the way she willingly touched you. I saw the way you spoke to her. The way you treated her."

"And that was enough to put your own life on the line?"

"What life?" she sneers, making my gut clench. "I was in the middle of being sold as a sex slave. My life was already over, and it didn't hurt that I could take out Burlone by backing your story."

The guilt that accompanies her bold assessment hits like a bull, making all the men in the room pause as they process it. She's right. And she was a genius for taking advantage of the opportunity that presented itself.

Once he's had a minute to digest the gravity of her situation, Kingston continues his questioning. "And what about now? You're free, yet you've put a giant target on your back. Those men are all being arrested for human trafficking, but that doesn't mean they don't know people who are still on the outside. They assume I'm going to kill you because you outed yourself as an agent, but Burlone sent your pictures to a lot of bad men. Men who possibly already had another buyer set in place in case they won the tournament. Men who could recognize you. Who could place you as an agent. Do you know what will happen if they find you?"

She doesn't move a muscle as he reams into her for putting her life in the crossfire. The irony isn't lost on me, though. Mr. Russo wouldn't have voted for Burlone's death if Q hadn't corroborated Kingston's story. Still, she deserves a better life than the one she's been dealt, and because of her sacrifice, it won't be getting easier anytime soon.

When she stays silent, Kingston keeps going. "If they

find you, the last two weeks of your life will have been a walk in the park compared to what they'll put you through. Understand?"

A single tear slides down her cheek, dripping off her chin and simultaneously showcasing an ounce of emotion from her otherwise comatose state. She doesn't bother to wipe it away.

"Enough," Diece barks, shocking the hell out of me.

All heads turn to him.

"Excuse me?" Kingston grits out.

"I'm pretty sure she gets the picture, Boss," D points out, his chest puffed up. "I think it's time you mention the solution now."

Kingston bristles at D's tone but shrugs it off for the time being as he orders, "My solution is for you to watch her, D. To take care of her until things calm down. Do you think you can do that? Keep her in hiding? Change her appearance? That kind of thing?"

With a mechanical nod, Diece's attention shoots to Q. She simply keeps staring blankly at the wall. Numb. As if her future isn't being discussed a few feet in front of her. As if she doesn't care what the outcome of her life will be because she's already given up on it.

And it's all my fault.

"Good. Ace," Kingston addresses her. "You're still living with me. Don't bother arguing."

"Who says I'm arguing?" she counters before crossing her arms.

With his lips tilted up in amusement, Kingston teases, "Good girl. Will you take Q up to the guest room across from us and make sure she's comfortable? D and I have a visitor we'd like to have a little chat with."

I notice my name isn't mentioned and assume I've been dismissed. Without waiting another second, I turn on my heel and leave the office.

But where am I going to go?

I have no clue.

CHAPTER TWENTY-NINE

REGINA

I'm alone. I don't know if it's a good thing or not because all I want to do is kick and scream. I want to cry. I want to hit something. I want to beg my brother to give Dex a chance. I can still hear his voice as he casually stated his verdict in reference to my happiness.

"And who is Regina Romano? She's the princess to the Romano family. She's the daughter of Gabriel and Emilia Romano and sister to Kingston Romano, the head of the Romano family. Now, let me ask you this. Who. Are. You?"

Doesn't the bastard know that there's more to me than my familial ties? I have hopes and dreams. I have wants and needs. And Dex? He's so much more than a name. He's kind. And funny. And protective. He's my everything.

Angrily, I wipe another tear from beneath my right eye before curling into a ball on my bed. It's funny, though. It doesn't feel like mine anymore. Not without Dex by my side.

I need to fix this. But how the hell do I do that?

Tossing and turning, I finally fall asleep a few hours later, the emotional day catching up with me. But that doesn't mean I'll forgive my brother for turning what should've been my happily ever after into a freaking nightmare.

* * *

A QUIET KNOCK against my bedroom door rouses me from my shitty sleep.

It's the decibel that gets to me, though. I live in a house full of brash mafia men. None of them knock quietly. I'm pretty sure they don't know how.

Tilting my head to the side, I unfold my legs from the bed and pad across the floor before hesitantly cracking the door open a few inches. When I see Ace, my best friend, the barbed barrier I'd been using as armor softens, and I invite her in.

"Hey," I mutter. A fresh wave of tears threatens to escape, and I blink them back.

The pity that greets me makes my chest ache before Ace pulls me into a hug.

"I'm so sorry," Ace apologizes into my tangled hair.

Shaking my head, I admit, "I hate him, Ace."

"Shh...," she coos before releasing me and making her way to my bed. Gingerly, she sits on the edge then motions me to follow. Once I'm seated beside her, she starts, "He's not trying to hurt you, G."

I laugh. "That's bullshit, and you know it. He's pissed that I snuck out and got caught. He's punishing me—"

"That's not true—"

"Yes, it is! You don't know him like I do, Ace. You don't understand our relationship. It's always been rocky."

"I…." Her face scrunches up, and I can tell I'm not going to like what she's about to say. "I think you'd be surprised how well I know him, Gigi. You've been gone for two weeks. I can only imagine the hell you've been put through, but I want you to know that you're not alone. Burlone spent years torturing me when I was a kid. If you need anyone to talk to or anything, I'm here for you. But like I said, you've been gone. Just like how I don't know exactly what you went through, you don't know what's been going on here, either. Your brother and me? We connected. Hard. And I fell for him, G. I love him."

I scoff, hating that I'm taking my anger out on her, but unable to help myself. "Good luck with that, Ace. He's an ass."

Her laughter surprises me. "He *is* an ass," she agrees. "But he has a good heart, and he's only looking out for you."

"If he cared about me, he'd let me be with Dex," I argue, my voice cracking as his name rolls off my tongue.

At the mention of my captor, Ace gulps and touches her side. I don't know if it's a subconscious reaction or not, but it still piques my curiosity.

"You've only known Dex for a short time, Gigi. I know you trust him and that he helped you, but maybe you don't know him that well and should give it some time…."

"Oh, the irony," I mutter under my breath.

"What's that supposed to mean?" she asks defensively, flinching as if I've slapped her.

Unable to help myself, I accuse, "You just admitted that you've only known my brother for a short amount of time, but you guys are living together now, and you have the audacity to tell me that I don't know Dex that well? Come on, Ace...you have to see the flaw in your logic."

Sighing, she tucks her hair behind her ear and looks toward the ceiling. "You're right. But you can't blame me for having trust issues with Dex."

"He sacrificed everything to help us," I point out.

"Yeah, but he also beat the shit out of me right before that."

"Wait, what?"

"I'm just saying...be careful. Give it some time."

"No." I shake my head. "What do you mean, he beat the shit out of you? You can't say something like that and not tell me exactly what you're talking about."

Rubbing her hand along her face, I can see the guilt that keeps her from filling me in.

"Tell me," I press.

With her lips sucked into her mouth, she eyes me warily.

"Tell me, Ace."

"After the tournament. The first one," Ace clarifies. Her shoulders hunch forward as she practically curls into a ball beside me like a scared little hedgehog.

"What happened?"

She clears her throat. "Burlone uh...he sent Dex to teach me a lesson."

Covering my mouth, the air gets caught in my lungs.

How did I not know about this?

"What kind of lesson, Ace?"

"I'm not saying it's his fault. I know he was only following orders and that Kingston has chosen to trust him. I'm just saying that I know what it's like to be on the

147

other end of his knuckles, and it doesn't feel so great. I don't blame Kingston for being a little hesitant to leave you with him without finding out if he's completely trustworthy first. That's all I'm saying."

"Dex would never hit me," I argue. "Trust me. I've seen what goes on under Burlone's supervision. Dex protected me. Over and over again, he protected me," I reiterate. "Hasn't he already proven he can be trusted?"

"Kingston thinks he can be trusted to be a Romano. The verdict is still up in the air as to whether or not he can be trusted with the Romano princess."

"You say that like Kingston hasn't already laid down the law."

"Rules can change, Gigi. That's all I'm saying." She grimaces before muttering under her breath, "And I probably shouldn't even say that much." Looking at me, she raises her voice a little louder. "You just need to be patient and cut your brother a little slack. Do you think you can do that?"

Chewing on my lower lip, I weigh my options. "Do I have a choice?"

"Not really," she teases dryly. "But if you really want Dex, then I suggest you try. For now, keep your distance from him. If Kingston thinks that Dex's loyalty isn't concrete, he won't make it out of here alive. Understand?"

I gulp. "Yeah. I understand."

CHAPTER THIRTY

DEX

A guy named Leo led me to a room in the back of the Romano estate after he found me wandering outside Kingston's office. It took me a second to recognize him, but I finally realized he's the same guy who watched me in the hallway the first day I met Kingston. However, he doesn't mention our initial introduction, and neither do I.

Located in the basement, with generic navy blue sheets and dark wood floors, I assume the room is standard living for lowly soldiers like myself. Regardless, once he points me to the private bathroom, I almost groan at the prospect of a shower.

Reading my mind, Leo orders, "Take a shower, and get some rest. We have a lot to discuss, but you need a clear head if we're going to put out all the fires that accompany a massive FBI raid followed by Burlone's disappearance. Stay here. Someone will come get you in a few hours."

Then he's gone.

And I'm left with a few hours to rethink my life and

my past mistakes that led me to a life without Regina by my side. But who am I kidding? A guy like me could never deserve a princess like her.

It's fucking torture.

* * *

Leo doesn't bother to knock.

Twisting the handle, he opens the door and sees me lounging on my bed with my forearm lying across my forehead as I try to catch a few minutes of shut-eye.

"Kingston wants to see you in his office."

I'm on my feet before he finishes his order. "Lead the way."

The walk is silent as we make our way up the stairs. The only sound that's heard is the occasional scuff of our shoes against the wood or a quiet creak in the floorboards as they take our weight.

With a flourish, Leo motions to Kingston's office. "In you go."

I knock against the door and wait to hear Kingston allow me to enter.

"Get in here, Dex."

As I step over the threshold, I'm surprised to find it almost empty other than Kingston sitting behind his desk with his phone in his hand.

"Where's D?" I ask, unable to help myself.

"He'll be hit or miss for the next little while, thanks to his current task," Kingston explains before setting his phone down. "Take a seat."

It's weird for me to be here, but I do as I'm told and pull out a leather cushioned chair across from Kingston's desk. Once I'm seated, Kingston dives right in. "You're going to be busy for a little while. Everyone knows you were one of Burlone's right-hand men. But the rumors have run rampant over the last twelve hours, and we need to make sure they're hearing *our* side of the story instead of dwelling on potential lies that seem to spread like wildfire."

"And what would you like them to know?"

"Exactly what we previously discussed. Burlone was working for the Feds. We narrowly managed to escape with Burlone before they stormed the estate where the tournament was being held and arrested Mr. Russo, Mr. Carbonne, Mr. Moretti, and the other gentlemen in attendance. We took care of Burlone, who died a traitor's death, and all of his dealings have now been passed on to you."

"Wait, what?"

"You heard me. Any dealings that Burlone was involved with have now fallen on your shoulders."

"But—"

He raises his hand. "Don't worry. We're done with Burlone's seedier activities, but they aren't going away on their own. We didn't go through all the shit in the last twenty-four hours only for someone else to step in and take over."

"Burlone's associates aren't going to be happy that orders have gone missing," I explain while attempting to hide my frustration. He's putting me in the middle of a damn war zone.

"No. They won't. But you have the Romano name behind you now, and if any of them have a problem with missing fruit, then you can send them to me. The fruit promised to them were taken in by the FBI, and we won't be collecting any more. It's non-negotiable."

They're not going to be happy about that. At all. But I can see Kingston's point. If we don't nip this in the bud, someone else will take over Burlone's kingdom, and we'll find ourselves in the same situation as before. And because of our previous decisions, there's chaos right now in the underground skin trade. I'm just not sure I can smooth things over.

Sensing my hesitation, Kingston presses, "There a problem, Dex?"

"I'll see what I can do," I concede as a heavy weight falls on my shoulders.

"Good." Pushing himself up from his seat, he rounds his desk and rests his hip against the edge of it. "Now, even though you've proven yourself to me, and I've made the informal announcement, a few of my associates would like to meet you in person and have suggested a"--he pauses in search of the right term--"more *formal* celebration to welcome you into the fold. I'll be inviting associates who had a connection with the Allegretti name to attend, as well. Will that be a problem?"

Squeezing the back of my neck, I shake my head. "No, sir."

"Good man." He pats me on the shoulder. "Stefan will go with you to corroborate your story when you meet with Burlone's associates." The threat is clear in his tone. I have a babysitter, and Kingston will be the first to know if I step out of line and spread any lies that don't coincide with Kingston's plan. Little does he know, it isn't necessary. I just want to leave my past behind me, along with the memories that continue to haunt me from my previous life. But apparently, that won't be happening anytime soon.

"That's fine," I answer him. "When is the celebration?"

"Soon. I also need you to recruit the trustworthy Allegretti men and to dispose of the untrustworthy."

"Dispose?"

His mouth quirks up on one side before disappearing just as quickly. "You'll be an assassin to our enemies as well as a delegate to our potential allies. Is that a problem?"

Shaking my head, I mutter, "No, sir."

"Good. Now, get out of here. Stefan already has the car pulled up to the front."

Pushing myself up from my chair, I leave with my mind reeling. If shit hits the fan, it'll be on me. Kingston's hands will remain clean.

I gotta give the bastard credit, though. He knows what he's doing. Now, I need to figure out my next move.

CHAPTER THIRTY-ONE

JACK

The pile of paperwork in front of me is mind-numbing. With a groan, I roll my shoulders and rock my head back and forth before hunching forward and reading over the confession another time. I still haven't gone home after arresting four of the top five human traffickers in the region. There's too much to sort through. Too many lies I need to make sure are hidden. Too many tracks to cover. And it's all because I made a deal with Kingston Romano and his girlfriend, Ace. Part of me wonders if I should regret my decision to give them false documents that incriminated Burlone to be working with the FBI. Then I look down at the images that were taken early this morning. A handful of girls' faces shine back at me. Some are pretty. Some aren't. Most are bruised and battered with a sloppy amount of makeup to cover the damage. But all of them are free now because I made a deal with the devil that prevented them from being sold.

So, no. I don't regret my decision one bit. I can't.

"Connelly!" my boss bellows down the hall, causing my head to snap up. Stalking through the doorway, he slams my office door behind him and stabs his forefinger at the images on my desk.

"You said you brought them all in!"

Brows furrowed in confusion, I reply, "I told you Burlone got away—"

"Not him! The girls! You said you brought all the girls! Some are missing! Where are the other girls?"

I shake my head, convinced I heard him wrong. "I'm sorry, what?"

"I didn't stutter, Connelly. Where are the other girls?" His face is red with anger. "And where the hell is Burlone?"

Probably dead, I think to myself before smoothing my expression and answering, "We're still searching for Burlone—"

"That's not good enough. Who are his contacts? Where did he go?!"

Frustrated, I slam my hand against my desk and stand to my full height. "We're doing the best we can. I haven't slept in almost thirty hours and am elbow deep in paperwork right now, but we're going to figure this out. You just need to give me a little more time."

"You've had enough time! Now, answer the damn question. Who wasn't arrested today that worked for Burlone? What do we know? And how can we find the other missing girls?"

"What do you mean, the other missing girls?" I ask, still misunderstanding how he would know that Ace and Kingston's sister got out of there before we showed up.

"Moretti's statement mentioned six girls. We only have four."

There were seven girls, I want to correct him. *He's missing Ace,* but I bite my tongue. I don't know what Kingston did with his sister, or the blonde that Moretti mentioned offhand in his statement, but it doesn't stop the walls from closing in. I'm gonna get caught. I'm gonna be raked over the coals for being a double agent when I was only trying to help.

I'm so screwed.

"We don't know where they went," I mutter.

"And do we know who's still out there with Burlone?"

"His right-hand men weren't brought in," I finally admit. Dex was never meant to be arrested. Kingston made sure I knew he wasn't supposed to be touched. And Sei, the other sonofabitch, wasn't on the premises when we stormed the estate. I have no freaking clue where he is.

"And do we know where they are?" Mr. Reed asks condescendingly.

We know where one of them is.

"No."

"Then find out. *Now.* And get me those girls."

"They're innocent. I assume they got out during the chaos. I doubt we'll be able to—"

"That's an order, Connelly," he sneers.

Then he's gone.

And I'm screwed.

CHAPTER THIRTY-TWO

REGINA

I haven't left my room. I don't want to. I'm still pissed, and despite what I'm sure my brother thinks, I'm not pouting, and I'm sure as hell not begging for his attention, either. I just can't deal with running into Dex, or Kingston, or even Ace right now. I just want to be alone.

Unfortunately, when I hear the brash knock against my bedroom door, I know who it belongs to, and I know he won't let me hide in here forever.

"What do you want?" I call out, instinctively knowing that it's my brother.

"Can I come in?"

I scoff. "Since when do you ask questions like that? You always do whatever the hell you want. Why stop now?"

The handle twists, and he comes into view before muttering, "I'll take that as a yes."

"Of course, you will," I quip.

With a sigh, he takes a step closer but continues to give me plenty of space at the same time. "Still pissed at me?"

"Are you surprised?"

"No." He rubs his hand down his face in defeat. "Look. I've been thinking a lot since you disappeared. I don't want you to feel like you're in a prison anymore. You've lived like that long enough."

My heart thrums in my chest like a hummingbird's wings, his comment taking me by surprise. "W-what do you mean?"

"I mean, I want you to have more freedom."

He can't be serious right now.

"The last time we tried that, I was kidnapped," I point out, though I have no idea why. Don't I want more freedom?

"We kept you hidden in hopes of keeping your identity anonymous. Once Burlone sent out that email with your picture, I think it dashed any hope of us going back to the original game plan. Which means we have a choice."

"And what choice is that?"

"Would you like to attend a gathering?" he mentions.

A gathering is basically a master networking party where different families gather together to connect, create alliances, transact business, and even form marital ties. They don't happen often, and I've always been ordered to hide away in my room like a dirty little secret whenever they've been held at our estate. Kingston's proposition to let me attend is...staggering.

Holding my breath, I blink a few times and try to register his words. "Y-you want me to go to a gathering?"

He nods. "Yes. I do."

"Why?"

With a dry laugh, he says, "I already told you. There's no putting you back in the bag now. You're out, Regina. And instead of trying to hide you all over again, I think we should own it. Let you be the queen you were born to be. Let them see that you're more than a weak girl hidden away in a tower somewhere."

My mind reels. "A queen?"

"Yeah. I'm not the only one who holds power in this family, Regina. You could own any man in that room, especially when they realize you're still on the market."

Aaand there it is––the catch.

"I'm not going to whore myself out for the family," I spit.

Holding up his hands in surrender, he states, "That's not what I meant—"

"Of course, it wasn't," I sneer, losing whatever respect I'd still had for the bastard. "I can't believe you'd come in here and say that to me! I love him, Kingston. But you've forbidden us from ever being happy together. Why would you do that?"

Pinching the bridge of his nose, he releases a sigh. "He's not good enough for you."

"Bullshit. In your eyes, no one will ever be good enough for me."

"You're right," he admits. "No one ever will be, but I'm going to do my best to make them rise to the challenge before I ever give you away, do you understand me?"

"I hear you loud and clear," I seethe.

"Good. I should probably give you a head's up. The gathering is for Dex. He'll be the star of the show. Do you think you can handle that?"

Tears pool in my eyes, and one slips out, sliding down

my cheek. My voice breaks as I ask, "And will all the desperate sluts be attending, as well?" It's common knowledge that these kinds of parties attract all the women who have yet to be married off. They swarm like hungry wolves, circling any new soldier like a piece of meat that needs to be tied down. My insecurities rear their ugly heads, quietly whispering that I'll never be enough to hold Dex's attention when we're already on shaky ground, and I cause so much more trouble than I'm worth.

The sound of Kingston's phone buzzing with a call prevents him from divulging which desperate women will be in attendance to distract the love of my life from remembering what we share together. Or shared. I'm not sure where he stands anymore. Not after he accepted Kingston's orders to leave me alone so easily. Does he even want me anymore?

With a finger raised at me, Kingston slides his thumb across the phone's screen and answers, "Why are you calling me, Jack?"

Silence.

"Our business is finished—"

A muffled voice on the other end cuts him off. His expression remains indifferent, but I can see a slight tick in his jaw that tells me he's close to snapping.

"Thank you for the update. I'll get back to you."

Ending the call, he turns back to me. "If you don't think you can handle the crowds, then don't come, but consider this your official invitation. I have to get going. Get some food and take a shower."

He storms out of the room seconds later, and I raise my arm, then take a whiff of my armpit. Yup. I totally need a shower. And I also need to figure out if I'm strong enough to see Dex swarmed by sluts from all sides.

Nope. Definitely not strong enough for that.

CHAPTER THIRTY-THREE

DEX

Stefan hits the lock button on his fob as we pull up to our current destination.

"Why are we here?" I ask as I take in the massive mansion with a wrap-around porch and a welcome mat by the front door.

"Lou traced an email that went to this IP address. It was in regards to Q's future...employer." His nose wrinkles in disgust while I read between the lines. Interesting. Sei had said that Burlone would let him keep Q for his own sick activities. Apparently, he'd been lying and had already set up a buyer. I'm not surprised that Burlone was going to fail in holding up his end of the bargain with Sei. I *am* surprised that he'd sell her to this man, though.

"Are you sure this is the right place?" I prod.

Stefan nods. "Yeah."

"Johnson has a kid. Do you know if he's home?"

Shaking his head, Stefan pulls out his phone and mutters, "Let me make sure. One sec."

I blow out a deep breath and wait for Stefan to do a bit

of research when my phone rings. After I pull it out, I answer, "Yeah?"

"How's it going?" Kingston asks.

"Fine," I grit out.

"Good. I just got a call from an...acquaintance. Apparently, the Feds are searching for Burlone's body."

"And what does that have to do with me?"

"It's in the back of your car." Tossing a glance over my shoulder, my eyes zero in on the trunk. "Well, that's...inconvenient."

"Or convenient, since I'd put it on Stefan's to-do list to dispose of it. Tell Stefan it needs to be more public than we'd initially anticipated. I'll also be sending you a number. I want you to give that number the location of his body so that we can be done with this. If the acquaintance has any more questions, he's going to contact you from now on. Understood?"

Piecing together the information Kingston just gifted me with, I realize that this acquaintance is likely the Fed who gave him the forged documentation that incriminated Burlone to be working with the enemy. I can also assume that by Kingston passing the buck to me, he's washing his hands and his connection, leaving me in the crosshairs in case anyone ever figures out our association with the FBI. Again.

Smart, Kingston. Very smart.

Not sure how much I like being the scapegoat for him, but any soldier would take the fall for their family, and I'm not any different. I just hope he'll start to recognize my loyalty as being absolute so that he finally gives me a chance with his sister.

I won't hold my breath, though.

"Yeah," I grunt. "I understand."

"Good."

The call disconnects. When I drop my arm back to my side, I see Stefan sauntering toward me. "Lou says the kid is at school today, so there shouldn't be any issues. Who were you talking to?"

"Kingston. Seems we have a friend in our trunk that needs disposing of after this."

Raising his chin in understanding, Stefan mutters, "Then let's get this shit taken care of."

And he walks past me, leaving me no choice but to follow.

* * *

As I rip a sheet off the king-sized bed, I notice Johnson's blood splattered across a family photo resting on the nightstand.

"How old is his kid?" I ask Stefan while examining the picture. I've only seen him a handful of times, but it had always been under circumstances where he was scared out of his mind, and he looked like a little mouse who was about to shit his pants. In the photo, he looks like a regular kid with mussed up hair and a wide smile. It's too bad his dad was a fucker who apparently liked to buy women on the side and needed to be disposed of. We couldn't have him sniffing around for his fruit, now could we? Regardless, I hope he has better luck than I did growing up, but I'm not betting any money on it.

Stefan shrugs. "I think Lou said ten."

Withholding my dry laughter, I toss the white sheet on top of the dead body strewn across the bedroom floor.

Of course, he is.

"Let's wrap him up then get out of here. I'll send a cleaning crew to wipe for prints, but I'm not sure we can do much about the soaked carpet."

"Yeah, blood's a bitch to get out," I agree.

Smirking, Stefan quips, "Kingston and Diece both say the same thing."

"That's 'cause they've done this a time or two." I lift Johnson's shoulder and tuck the sheet beneath the life-taking wound in the back of his skull to prevent any more blood from dripping all over the floor. Stefan gets on the opposite side, lifting his legs while I grip under his armpits.

Man, this asshole is heavy.

"So...how long have you been in the family?" I ask, making conversation.

"A while. I heard about the flashy party they're throwing you, by the way. Usually, they only hold them for the bigwigs, or they wait until there's a big enough group of soldiers being welcomed into the fold to justify the chaos. You nervous?"

With a shrug, I guide us out the bedroom door and down the stairs to the first floor. "I don't know. Should I be?"

"Meh." He mirrors my earlier movement and shrugs. "You'll be fine. Just be careful who you talk to."

"What do you mean?"

"Every man there is trying to marry off their daughter. If you're caught looking at one for too long, or even offer a generic smile to the wrong, desperate girl, they'll be all over you like white on rice trying to pawn themselves off."

Grimacing, I glance over my shoulder to make sure I

don't run into anything as I walk down the stairs backward.

"I heard Kingston invited Regina," Stefan continues.

Hearing her name amplifies the dull ache in my chest. "Yeah?"

"Yeah."

"Is that out of the norm for her to attend one of these things?"

"Yeah. The Allegrettis were blacklisted, which is why you never attended a gathering, but Regina was always tucked away in her room to prevent anyone from snapping a picture to reveal her true identity."

"Since that strategy worked so well in the first place," I add sarcastically before stepping out into the morning air. The body swings from side to side as we approach the car.

Stefan chuckles with me. "Pretty much."

"Hmmm," I hum. Dropping the corpse onto the ground, I open the back door to keep any of his blood from touching Burlone, then we shove him in the back seat. Wouldn't want any cross-contamination or anything.

Once he's situated, Stefan gets behind the steering wheel, and I slide into the front seat before he asks, "So did you know the guy well?"

I look over my shoulder to the stained sheet.

"Yeah," I breathe.

"How 'bout his son?"

Shaking my head, I admit, "I don't know him well, but I've seen him a few times. Johnson was an outlier. He didn't have a connection to the family, initially. Hell, he approached Burlone about a year ago and slowly weaseled his way into making connections. I've never heard of him purchasing a girl, though, but his son was being groomed for the family."

"They start young, don't they?"

"We all start young. Well"—I give him the side-eye —"most of us. What the hell made you want to join the Romanos?"

Mouth quirking, he confides, "You and I aren't that different, Dex. We were both raised in shit homes with shit moms. I realized how much I needed a family to watch my back, so I went searching for them."

"Is that what the Romanos do?" I quip, unable to hide my disbelief. "Watch each other's backs?"

"Yeah. They do. And once you're initiated with the gathering, they'll officially have yours too."

And I want that so much that it hurts. But I want Regina more. The real question is, will I be able to have my cake and eat it too?

Turning my attention back to the road, I mutter, "I guess we'll see."

And all the while, an image of my Little Bird haunts me because I feel like if I have my brothers, then I'll lose something that's so much more important to me.

WE TAKE care of Burlone's burial first because it's more crucial we don't leave any evidence of Johnson on Burlone's body than if Johnson ends up with a little of Burlone's blood on him. Why? Because Kingston ordered me to disclose the location of Burlone's body to a Fed, and we don't want it connected to Johnson's disappearance in any way, shape, or form.

Although, as I look at Burlone's decrepit body, a part of me wonders if anyone would be able to recognize him if we didn't hand out the exact location of his corpse. Half his skull is missing, and what little is left of his face is bloated and black and blue. Hell, he was practically my pseudo dad, even if he was a shitty one, and I'd have a hard time placing his identity.

Hopefully, it'll be enough to satisfy the Feds and get them off our asses now. I guess we'll find out.

I check the text from Kingston and type in the number he'd forwarded to me. It rings three times before a foreign voice answers, "Hello?"

"It's in the woods off 49th and Emerson Road. You'll see a giant oak and freshly churned ground. Good luck."

Then I disconnect the call and rub my hand across my face.

"You okay, man?" Stefan asks from the driver's seat.

"Just tired."

Turning on his blinker, he heads toward the location of where he'd initially told me we'd be disposing of Johnson's body. "Then let's get this shit done and go home."

A comfortable silence encompasses the cab as the trees on both sides of the road blur past us. After a few minutes, Stefan breaks it with, "I uh, I wanted to thank you, by the way."

"For what?" I ask, keeping my gaze on the lush greenery outside.

"For taking care of Regina. I was tasked with watching her, and I failed. Without you, she never would've made it out of there."

His compliment makes me pause, and I rest my head against the headrest behind me, contemplating the validity of it. Would she have made it out of there? Did she really need me? And did I end up saving her, or was it the other way around?

"I did what I could," I admit on a sigh. "But I'm not sure if I crossed the line or not in the process."

"You mean by sleeping with her?" Stefan suggests.

My eyes pop open in surprise, but I don't deny it.

"Regina doesn't do anything she doesn't want to do, man. Trust me. I've seen it firsthand. She likes you, and I don't think you should discount that. Neither should Kingston. Now, we just have to wait and see how it all plays out."

I roll my eyes, unable to hide my annoyance. "We already know how it's going to play out."

"We'll see," he says ominously.

And I leave it at that.

CHAPTER THIRTY-FOUR

REGINA

y stomach grumbles, finally getting the best of me until I find myself with my back to the kitchen in front of an open fridge showcasing my snack options. Feeling weirdly indecisive about what sounds good, it hits me.

I hadn't been able to choose what I wanted to eat for two weeks. Dex simply brought me whatever was available, and I ate it. Things started bland, like the cool soup and tepid water. But soon, Dex was sneaking in Snickers bars and M&M's in hopes of making me smile while attempting to help me forget about my crappy circumstances for a minute.

And it worked.

Angry, I slam the fridge closed and turn toward the stairway, determined to go sulk in my room a little longer when I run straight into a chest.

A warm, hard chest that smells a little woodsy with a side of—

"What the hell are you doing out here?" Dex's gruff voice scolds.

With my hands pressed against his pecs, I look up and nearly crumble before realizing the guy in front of me is pissed. And I have no idea why.

"Excuse me?"

"What are you doing out here?" he repeats, trying to soften his tone by removing his initial curse from the question.

"I was hungry...." My voice trails off when I realize his hands are resting against my hips, pinning me in place.

"Do you always walk around here dressed like that?"

Looking down, I find myself in a soft, white T-shirt and a pair of sleep shorts. If I'm being honest, he's seen me in a hell of a lot less.

"Dressed like what?" I question, peeking back up at him.

With a shake of his head, his jaw tightens. "I can see your fucking nipples, Regina, which means every other soldier in this house can too."

I look down at my chest, and sure enough, they're standing at full attention.

Oops....

Still, his tone makes me bristle, fanning the flames of bitterness that have been threatening to take hold ever since he let me walk out of Kingston's office without bothering to fight for me.

"I'm sorry, what the hell is your problem?" I spit.

His fingers tighten against me. "Nothing."

"Bull crap. You can't storm in here pissed at me for no reason. You can't make me feel like shit for wearing a freaking T-shirt in my own home. You can't give me that cold look that reminds me of our nights together when I wasn't sure if I'd make it out alive or not. You can't—" A sob escapes me, cutting off my stupid chastising as I bury my face into his chest.

Whoa...emotions.

"Shh...."

I feel his chest rumble beneath my cheek, but it doesn't stop the tears from falling.

"Where have you been?" I choke out now that the dam has finally broken. "Why didn't you come see me? Did I really mean that little to you? Why didn't—"

"Hell no, Little Bird. Don't assume shit with me, okay? I'm begging you."

"What else can I assume?" I cry, my entire body shaking like a leaf in the wind. I feel like I'm going to blow away. That I'm going to crumble beneath the pressure from someone's boot as soon as I hit the ground. But the tree that'd been protecting me has let me go, despite my desperation to cling to it, and my descent is inevitable.

"Shh...," he breathes, wrapping his arms around my lower back and pressing our fronts together. His fingers tangle in my hair, tugging at the roots as they massage my scalp in slow, deliberate circles.

It feels amazing, but I need answers more than I need his touch.

"Answer me," I grit out, hating how weak I sound. I've never been weak. I'm the pain in the ass little sister to Kingston Romano. I'm the princess of a freaking mafia family. I'm the get-shit-done, go-in-guns-blazing kind of girl. But all of that seems to be stripped bare as I stand in front of a man who owns every piece of me.

And doesn't seem to care in the slightest.

When he's still silent, I repeat, "I said, answer me."

"I love you, Little Bird."

My chest tightens, and my fingers dig into his rumpled white shirt in an attempt to keep him from leaving me again.

"Then why are you letting my brother keep us apart?"

"I'm not," he argues, tightening his hold. His chin brushes against the top of my head as I feel him shake his head back and forth. "I'm not, okay? But your brother's right. You're too good for me, Regina. I'm no one. I'm nothing. I need to make my place here so that I can earn a right to call you mine. Right now, I don't deserve to wipe the shit off your shoes. Especially after what I put you through."

"How can you say that?" My voice cracks again, and I hate how desperate I sound.

"Do you know what I did today?" he asks, practically giving me whiplash from his abrupt subject change. "I killed a guy. I killed a guy who had a ten-year-old kid."

When the age dawns on me, I want to cry. "The same age you were...."

"Yeah. The same age I was when my entire world got ripped apart, and look what I just did? I gave the kid the same future as the one that was mapped out for me. These hands?" He drops them from my waist and steps away from me. "They ruined a kid's life today. How the hell do you think they deserve holding you after what they've done? Do you know how many other people I have to hunt down because of the mess with Burlone, and how it might look with Kingston being the only boss to walk away? It's a lot, Regina. But, I never cared before. I never gave a shit about any of them because I knew I only had to think about myself and my selfish ass. But now, there's you. The sweet, sexy-as-hell girl who's so far out of my league that I'm left scrambling because I want you with every fiber of my being, but you'll always be just out of reach."

The distance nearly breaks me, leaving me no choice but to rush forward and tangle our fingers together.

"What have I told you about these hands?" I cry. "They were made for me. They were made to hold me. To protect me. To care for me. Without them, I don't even know what to eat anymore. Why can't you see that?" Dragging my quivering lips against his busted-up knuckles, I press open-mouthed kisses to each of them.

"Please," I whisper. "Don't let my brother define my future. Let me choose my own path. Let me choose you." Keeping his hands pressed against my lips, I squeeze my eyes shut. The tears stream down my cheeks and drip onto his closed fists. But it's his presence that seems to calm my frantic soul. His ever-sturdy frame as it towers over me. Making me feel small. But precious. His lips caress my forehead in a soft kiss that turns my insides into Jell-O.

"Come here, Little Bird."

I'm not sure I can get much closer, but I inch forward until the leather of his loafers tickles my bare toes.

"Look at me," he orders.

I shake my head. I can't right now. Not when I've bared my soul to him without knowing how he'll respond.

"I said, look at me, Little Bird." The commanding tone leaves me no choice but to pull my lids open. Resting my chin against our tangled fingers, I look up at him to find him staring down at me. The room is dark, having lost the only light from the refrigerator after I slammed it shut, but I can still see the shadow of the man I love shrouded in darkness. It's fitting and reminds me of our nights together in that cold, dank basement with only a single bulb hanging from a wire as our source of light. With my recent history, I should probably be terrified and suffer a mental breakdown from the flashback. But I'm not scared when he's around. I just wish he could see what I do when I look at him.

"I will never be good enough for you, regardless of what your brother thinks, or approves of."

"And I will never care about what you do when you're away from me as long as you always come back and stop punishing yourself for the shit you have to do," I counter.

His breath fans across my face, inching closer until I'm positive he'll put me out of my misery and release the vise he'd wrapped around my chest since the moment I stormed out of my brother's office. Licking my lips, I raise up onto my tiptoes and—

"What the hell are you two doing?" Stefan interrupts. He keeps his voice low to prevent others from hearing, but his disapproval is apparent. As he flips the light switch on the wall, I squint and feel like I'm in the middle of being interrogated. Like I've been caught doing something that I'm not supposed to even when it's the only time I actually feel like I'm doing something right with my life.

Dex, on the other hand, jumps back as if he's been burned.

"Nothing," he grunts before running his palm across his face. "I was just leaving."

"And I was just getting some food, but apparently, I'm not very hungry anymore."

Leaving Dex on his own, I step around Stefan and climb up the stairs to my room. I can't deal with Dex if he doesn't want to fight for me and what we could have together.

What we *did* have before we lost it all.

CHAPTER THIRTY-FIVE

DEX

I watch Regina walk away, her long legs creating more distance between us with every step. The memory of what her silky skin felt like wrapped around my waist, combined with the knowledge that I'm unable to chase her the way I want to, pisses me off. My entire body buzzes with adrenaline, and I take a step toward her without even thinking about it when Stefan grabs my forearm.

"Don't."

"Fuck off," I growl.

He doesn't release me. "Look, man. I'm rooting for you guys, okay? Seriously, I am. But I also know that Kingston will put you in the ground if you disobey his orders, especially when I'm pretty sure it's just a test to confirm where your loyalties lie." His mouth forms a thin line before he continues. "Just…be patient. That's all I'm saying."

"Be patient for what?" I sneer. "No matter how much time or sacrifices I put in under the Romano name, I'll never be good enough for Kingston's baby sister."

With a grin, he answers, "You're right. You won't. But Kingston is a generous bastard and might take pity on you, anyway, if you keep your head down and do what you're told. Besides"—he loses his smile—"if you slip up, and Kingston is forced to exact retribution on your ass, who do you think it's going to hurt most?"

The answer is simple, but I can't voice it aloud.

After seeing me come to the conclusion that Regina would be caught in the crosshairs, he raises his chin and confirms, "Exactly. The gathering is tomorrow. Are you ready for that?"

"For what, exactly? The only parties Burlone ever held were basically orgies with a side of prostitution."

Letting go of my arm, he explains, "Sometimes they feel more like a speed dating event than anything else. You're going to be fresh meat down there. And so is Regina."

"She's really going?" He'd mentioned it before, but I hadn't pieced together that men will swarm her the same way Stefan is positive women will swarm me.

He nods. "Yeah. Kingston is trying to patch things up with her by granting her some freedom where he actually has some control over the situation and everyone it involves. It's his own proverbial olive branch, but I think you should be warned that things might get…." His voice trails off, and I find myself anxious to hear him finish his sentence.

"Might get…what?" I bite out.

"For lack of a better word, I'm going to go with *interesting*. No one has seen her since her mom died over a decade ago. I won't be surprised if people start pulling out their phones and snapping pictures like she's Big Foot or something. As far as I know, Kingston has backed off on the whole betrothal thing, but that doesn't mean that every single available man in the room won't be attempting to mark her as theirs. Do you think you can witness that without intervening?"

Though I keep my expression blank, he can still feel the heated energy rolling off me as I imagine witnessing a bunch of vultures swarm my Little Bird.

"Just...be ready," Stefan advises. "And don't lose your head or you might *literally* lose your head. Understand?"

I keep my mouth shut because I can't guarantee shit right now.

Taking my silence as confirmation, he adds, "Good. Now, go get some sleep. We had a long day."

* * *

I SLEEP LIKE SHIT. My legs get tangled in the navy blue covers as I toss and turn. All the while, my mind runs on repeat, contemplating my life and how everything got so screwed up. I always assumed all my issues stemmed from working for the bad guys. My mouth quirks up in amusement.

Yeah, like the Romanos are a bunch of saints.

Fed up, I rip the sheets away from me, then head upstairs in a pair of basketball shorts and nothing else. I feel like this night will never end. The smell of coffee tickles my nostrils as I round the corner to the kitchen. Digging my heels into the dark wood floors beneath me, I stop short when I recognize the culprit behind the warm caffeine's aroma wafting through the air.

"Oh," I grumble before turning on my heel.

"Wait!" Ace calls out when she sees me.

Positive I've heard her wrong, yet unable to help myself, I freeze.

"I just made some coffee," she murmurs behind me. "Do you want some?"

With my heart pounding against my ribcage, my feet move on their own until I find myself facing her again. In a dark kitchen. While everyone else is sound asleep.

The irony isn't lost on me, and I almost drown in the tsunami of regret when it hits me square in the chest.

"Uh…sure," I mutter, feeling awkward as hell.

After giving me a kind smile, she stands on her tiptoes and reaches for a second mug before pouring coffee into it. When I notice her splash a bit onto the counter, I realize she's shaking. And it's all because of me.

Shit.

I can feel her anxiety rolling off her in waves, though she does her best to hide it.

"Hey, uh…Ace?"

"Mmmhmm?" she hums, but she doesn't look over at me. Her attention is glued to the swirling granite countertop.

"Can you wait here for just a second?"

Bringing her cup to her lips, she swallows a big gulp of coffee before nodding, though she refuses to look me in the eye.

I take the stairs two at a time down to my room then rummage through a duffle bag I'd tossed into the corner. When I find what I'd been looking for, I race back up to the kitchen, shocked to see that Ace actually listened to my request and stuck around for a minute.

In an effort not to startle her, I keep my movements

slow and deliberate. Placing a wrinkled cashier's check next to her cup, I make sure not to set it in the spilled coffee from when she'd attempted to pour me some.

"What's this?" she asks, her voice almost squeaking in surprise when she realizes what it is. Her hands remain tight on her cup like she's afraid to reach out and touch it.

"It's your winnings from the tournament," I answer her.

"But—"

"You earned it."

Licking her lips, she peeks up at me through her thick, dark lashes before finding the courage to set down her cup and touch the worn piece of paper that she sacrificed everything for. Ace drags her trimmed fingernail along the amount typed onto the check, her coffee seemingly forgotten as she inspects it closely.

"Umm...." She releases a shaky breath. "Thank you."

Scratching the scruff along my jaw, I search for my own courage to finally voice an apology that's been brewing inside of me since the moment Burlone gave me my orders to beat the shit out of her.

"Hey, Ace?"

She looks up at me. "Yeah?"

"I'm uh...." I rock back on my heels. "I'm sorry for what I did."

She forces a tight smile onto her face before shrugging one shoulder. "It's fine."

"It's not fine," I argue, hating myself a little more that she would even consider using *fine* as a way to describe what I did to her. "Ace, listen to me. I was a coward for not standing up to Burlone like I should've. I've done a lot of shitty things in my life, but hurting you was hands

181

down one of the most despicable out of all of them. I was born a survivor, and survivors will do a lot of shady shit to make it to the next day. But hurting you? It was unacceptable, and I promise I won't let anyone ever order me to do something like that ever again."

"I'm a survivor, too, Dex. I get it. I think we all live with regrets in our lives. Part of me wonders if it was my fault that Gigi was taken. Sure, she's Kingston's sister, but maybe she wouldn't have tried to sneak out that night if I hadn't been dumb enough to enter that tournament in the first place. Maybe she wouldn't have had any desire to sneak out if I'd never sat down with her at Dottie's and sparked a friendship. Maybe—"

"It's not your fault, Ace," I console, unable to listen to her question her actions that might've led to a different outcome. It's a dangerous rabbit hole that she shouldn't go down.

"And following orders when that's all you've ever known," she clarifies, "isn't entirely your fault, either."

"I'm so fucking sorry," I reiterate.

With another kind smile, she picks up the mug she'd initially poured for me and nudges it toward me.

"I forgive you, Dex. And, hopefully, we can both learn from our past mistakes and maybe even figure out when to follow our own hearts instead of someone else's orders, ya know?"

My suspicion spikes as I register her comment before brushing it off as a coincidence. There's no way she suggested I ignore Kingston's order to stay away from Regina. It'd be like signing my own death warrant while stabbing my Little Bird in the heart while I'm at it. I can't do that to her.

Bringing the cup to my mouth, I let the bitter liquid wash over me before adding, "I know the likelihood of you ever trusting me is slim at best, but you have me, Ace. If you ever need anything, it's yours."

Her mouth quirks on the corner, only this time it's genuine. "So, like…you owe me a favor or something?"

With an awkward laugh, because I have no idea where she's going with this, I confirm, "I guess so?"

"Noted. Can I claim it right now?"

Gaze narrowing in suspicion, I repeat, "I guess so?"

"Good. Don't hurt Gigi 'cause she deserves the world. And while you're at it, don't piss off Kingston, either."

And I guess there's my answer. If I disobey Kingston's orders, it'll definitely piss him off. Guess that means I'll need to keep being a good little rule follower.

I just hope Regina will be patient with me while I sort out this messed up situation and figure out how to give her everything she deserves.

CHAPTER THIRTY-SIX

REGINA

*M*y entire body is humming with anticipation. Or maybe it's nerves. Maybe it's annoyance. I can't really put my thumb on it, but I do know that I want to throw up as I lean against the counter in my bathroom and swipe the mascara wand along my upper lashes one more time.

Hearing a soft knock on my bedroom door, I call out, "Yeah?"

"It's me," a feminine voice responds.

"Come in."

My hair is pulled to the side, hanging over my right shoulder in soft waves. Even though it looks fine, I run my fingers through it and tease the roots a little more to give it some body.

"You look great," Ace compliments as she peeks through the doorway.

"Thanks," I mutter before checking her out. "Uh... speaking of looking great. Day-um, Ace. You look awesome."

Her cheeks heat as she tucks a strand of hair behind her ear. "Thanks. I don't really know what to expect with this whole shindig tonight. What's it like?"

Snorting, I reply, "You're asking the wrong girl. I've never been to one of these, either."

"Seriously?"

"Yup. Depressing, huh?"

"I'm just surprised. Kingston said it's kind of a big deal."

I laugh. "It is. Surrounding families and associates come from all over to attend, but I was never allowed to go because my dad wanted to keep my identity hidden."

"Your brother may have mentioned that part," Ace admits with a look of pity. "But look at the bright side. Now, we both get to pop our mafia party cherries together." She bounces her perfectly shaped eyebrows up and down for good measure.

With a giggle, I concede, "Touché. It'll definitely be interesting. I've been so isolated from everyone that I don't really know what to expect, either. I've only heard stories."

"Yeah. Kingston said there'll be wine, finger foods, and business suits. And that my mind will be spinning by the end of it. Oh! And he said that I shouldn't stress if I don't remember anyone's name by the end of it because—"

"Because you're Kingston's future wife, and they'll be too afraid to correct you," I quip with a smile.

Blushing, she waves me off. "Let's not get ahead of ourselves."

"Uh...you don't know how the families work. It's all about marriage, and connections, and business deals, and blah, blah, blah. Just make sure you don't let Kingston out of your sight. Until you put a ring on his finger, the sharks will still consider him free game and will be circling him like a bunch of hungry piranhas."

Her eyes widen. "What do you mean?"

"These gatherings are also a prime event for finding spouses, which is why I've never really cared whether I was invited to attend. It's also why I wasn't invited, now that I think about it." I laugh. "My dad didn't want me to come out until it was on the arm of my future husband."

"Well…I mean…Dex will be there, too, right?" Ace offers, trying to look at the bright side.

"Yeah. And he'll be seen as fresh meat. Most of the girls wouldn't even dream of ending up with a mob boss. But a sexy soldier like Dex is definitely within their reach." I sigh before running my fingers through my hair all over again. Ace grabs my hands to stop them from fussing and gives me a quick squeeze to make sure she has my attention.

"Be patient, G. I already told you—"

"I know! But…part of me wonders if that's Kingston's plan. To introduce him to a bunch of eligible bachelorettes on a smorgasbord, and he can go crazy with whoever he wants. What if…." I blink back my emotions. "What if he forgets about me or realizes that he could have any girl in that room?"

"Gigi," she sighs. "Don't think about it like that. Dex would be lucky to have you, and I know for a fact that he wants you and *only* you. Don't shrug off his feelings just because you're scared about how strongly you feel for him."

If my feelings are that apparent to her, then why can't my brother see it?

"I'll try, Ace. I promise I'll try."

"Good. And if shit hits the fan downstairs, I've got your back."

"Ditto."

The bustle from the main floor filters into my suite, amplifying my nerves all over again.

"You ready to go?" Ace asks, watching me closely.

"As ready as I'll ever be."

"Good. Because now that you've mentioned the sharks, I'm a little worried to leave Kingston down there by himself."

I laugh. "Trust me. You have nothing to worry about. He only has eyes for you."

"And Dex only has eyes for you," she counters.

"I guess we'll see."

CHAPTER THIRTY-SEVEN

REGINA

y deep red heels match my sleeveless dress perfectly, and I find myself thanking the designer gods who were smart enough to add a slit that reaches my mid-thigh. Without it, there's no way I'd be able to walk down the stairs from my room to the first floor. My hand clutches Ace's as I feel multiple sets of eyes on me. With my gaze glued to my red heels, I take a deep breath.

I can't decide if they're looking at me, the princess of the Romano family, or if they're looking at Ace, the woman who captured the Dark King's heart. Or maybe I'm imagining their stares all together, and it's entirely in my head. I chance a glance toward a long table that's tucked against the wall where a group of guests has congregated together. Each and every one of them is turned in our direction. Some have open curiosity in their gazes. Others seem unamused with our presence. And a few look like they've eaten something sour.

When I see Dex's face mingled with the rest, my steps

falter. A girl is clinging to his forearm like a little monkey as she throws her head back, laughing.

My spine straightens as I debate on running back to my room when Ace's grip tightens.

"He's not interested in her, G. He's staring at you."

Squeezing my eyes shut, I take a deep breath, then open them and search for my protector. When our gazes connect, I watch his jaw tighten, but he doesn't move a damn muscle.

"He might be staring at me," I mutter under my breath, "But he hasn't shrugged away from her, either."

"Be patient, G. That's all I'm saying," she replies before leading me the rest of the way to the first floor. I don't like that I've lost my vantage point of the room, but there's nothing I can do about it.

After ushering me to the side of the room for a little space to breathe, Ace grabs two glasses of wine from a server and shoves one into my hand.

"Here. Liquid courage."

"I'm Italian," I counter. "Which means I'm gonna need an entire bottle."

Grinning, she quips, "Challenge accepted." Then she's gone, and I'm left with a house plant for company with a side of staring from every single person in the room.

I spot Dex through the crowd in his pristine black tux with his short, dark hair slicked back. There's still a bit of scruff on his face, though, and I kind of love the tiny act of rebellion that accompanies it. If only the X tattoo on his forearm was on display, then I'd be transported back to when we first met, and I could keep him all to myself. Feeling my inspection, his eyes meet mine like a homing beacon before the same girl from moments ago appears beside him. I watch her mouth graze the shell of his ear as she whispers something to him, but the sight quickly disappears when a man in a navy blue suit steps in front of me.

"Regina, I presume?" he asks.

"And you are…?" I return in a cool tone.

"Alessandro Marino. I was a friend of your father's before he passed."

Obviously, I want to say, but I keep my snark to myself and ask, "Is that right?"

The name sounds vaguely familiar, and I take my time assessing him a little more closely. He has dark hair and a soft build around the center, not appearing to be over-weight by any means, but I can tell he doesn't spend his time at the gym or doing anything particularly active, either. Tilting my head, I notice that he's maybe a few inches taller than me if I'm not wearing heels, but today we're practically the same height. It's his eyes, though, that get to me. Icy blue and just as cold.

"Yes. I apologize that he never had a chance to formally introduce us."

There's something about the way he says it that causes the hair along my arms to stand on end. Brushing my open palms along them, I rock back on my heels and mutter, "Yes. Quite a pity. Excuse me, but––"

"Already running along?" he asks, following my retreat by taking a step closer. His movement nearly pins me against the wall behind me, and my fight or flight instinct threatens to rear its ugly head.

"Well, I—"

"Regina! There you are," a deep voice calls from a few feet away. Alessandro's and my head swivels in the same direction to see a stranger stalking closer. I've never seen him before, but that isn't exactly surprising given my history. However, when his mouth stretches into a secret smile, I know that I'm going to like him.

"I believe you owe me a dance." He offers his arm, and I catch myself taking it without a second thought. I'd do anything to get away from the creeper, and this stranger seems like the best kind of distraction to battle my woes with Dex, so I'm going to call it a win-win.

Leading me to the dance floor, he spins me into his arms then shifts his weight from one foot to the other while keeping a respectable amount of distance between us. The space earns him a few extra brownie points too.

"I'm Matteo, by the way," he introduces himself with a mischievous smirk. "Looked like you needed a little help back there."

I don't miss the fact that he doesn't mention his last name. It's peculiar, to say the least. Especially in a setting like this where the weight of a last name can crush adversaries. After a moment of hesitation, I decide to let it go.

"I did, actually. Thanks."

"Don't mention it."

"I'm Regina," I add, remembering my manners. I mean, I know *he* knows my name, but it still feels weird that I didn't officially introduce myself.

He grins. "I know."

The heat from his hand as it rests against my lower back is...weird. It's apparent he's making sure to only touch my mid-back, but still. No one has ever touched me like this. Except Dex. My chest tightens as I peek over Matteo's shoulder in search of him and his floozy in a red dress.

I glance down at the dress I'm wearing that matches the bimbo's in color. My expression sours, causing a deep chuckle to reverberate through my dance partner.

"You okay there?"

"Mmhmm," I hum through pursed lips.

"You sure? 'Cause you just gave your dress—that looks beautiful on you, by the way—a glare that would make a grown man cower in fear."

With a light laugh, I roll my eyes before admitting, "It's nothing."

"You're a terrible liar, Regina," he points out. "But I'll let it go for now."

"That's very kind of you."

"Not usually a term that's used to describe me, but I'll take it. Besides, we're in the mafia. Our entire world is built on secrets, is it not?" He spins me around before pulling me back into his arms and dipping me low.

"It is," I concur when my feet are firmly on the ground, and we go back to gently swaying.

"Tell me this," Matteo prods. "Does your secret have something to do with a big, brooding man over there?" His gaze shoots over my shoulder before he spins me around so that I can take a peek without seeming too conspicuous.

When I see Dex glaring at me, I mutter, "Ding, ding, ding. We have a winner."

"Interesting. Can I also assume that your little vendetta against your dress might have something to do with Bianca Castello, who wore a matching color and happened to be hanging on him earlier tonight?"

"Castello?"

He nods.

"As in...Dominic Castello?" The name leaves a sour taste in my mouth. My dad approached me before he died and mentioned finding me a potential spouse before I lost my shit on him. Thankfully, he bailed on the idea before seeing it come to fruition, but I'll never forget the bastard's name.

"Bianca is Dominic's younger sister, though I'm a bit confused as to why they were invited."

"What do you mean?" I ask, growing more and more fascinated by Matteo the longer I spend my time in his presence. Seems to me that he's a keeper of secrets. Yet, here he is, divulging them to me. A woman.

"There're rumors that he was in bed with Burlone. Not literally," he clarifies with a crooked smirk. "But he was definitely invested in the Allegretti name. Then again, so was your boy."

I lick my lips but don't comment, praying he'll feel generous and continue his musings.

"Would you like to hear my theory?" he asks, watching me with open curiosity.

I nod while taking in the laugh lines around his soft green eyes.

"I think it's a power play. Your brother is showing that he isn't afraid of the Allegretti name. That he dethroned Burlone from power and can easily do it again to anyone who stands against him."

"You're perceptive," I compliment, albeit grudgingly. "What else have you observed?"

"That you've already won the hearts of every available man in this room, though yours seems to have been stolen for some time."

I swallow but don't bother to deny it.

"Who are you?" I repeat, my voice laced with awe.

"A friend, if you ever need it."

"To me? Or the Romano family?" I press.

"Both." Spinning me a second time, he pulls me in close then murmurs, "Tell me, Regina. The man who's stolen your heart is currently contemplating how he can make my death look like an accident. Would you like me to continue our charade that's making him question his sanity, or should we put him out of his misery?"

I sneak a quick peek over Matteo's shoulder then lick my lips. "I guess I should probably go talk to him."

With a soft shake of his head, Matteo leans closer and whispers in my ear. "Excuse yourself from the room. I guarantee he'll follow, and you'll be able to find a bit more privacy. As I'm sure you can see, you won't find it in here with all of these guests who are watching your every move."

He's right.

I nod my assent before my mouth stretches into a smile as I realize that I actually enjoyed our little interaction. "Thank you for asking me to dance."

"Thank you for accepting the invitation instead of making me look like a fool in front of a fellow associate," he returns with a knowing grin. "Alessandro is an ass, but he's harmless."

"Good to know. I'll uh…I guess I'll see you around."

My heels click against the floor as I make my escape, though I can feel more than one set of eyes on me as I do so. When I round the corner and find a bit of privacy, I clutch my chest and look around to find it empty.

"What the hell was that?" Dex spits seconds later, grabbing my forearm. Tugging me into the closest room, he slams the door shut then shoves me up against the nearest wall.

"Excuse me?" I reply, just as frustrated. "What the hell was what?"

"That"—he waves his giant hand toward the room where the party is being held—"dance, or whatever the hell it was. He was all over you!"

A dry laugh bursts out of me as I roll my eyes. "Are you serious right now? He was an absolute gentleman–– unlike Bianca Castello," I spit her name like it's a curse.

Shaking his head, his hands tighten on my hips until I'm sure they'll leave tiny bruises on my skin. But I look forward to seeing them. It'll remind me that, at one time, I was able to pull enough passion out of the enigma in front of me that he couldn't control himself.

"I don't want Bianca," he growls.

"Could've fooled me."

"That's bullshit, and you know it."

"Then why did you let her touch you?" I seethe.

"Because I needed information."

I shove him away, but he barely budges. "Is that what they're calling it these days?"

Shaking his head, he spits, "You're one to talk, Regina. For a girl who claims she loves someone, you seemed pretty entertained with Matteo fucking Moretti."

"What?" His last name leaves me spinning.

"Yeah. Does the name sound familiar, Little Bird? Or maybe you just have a thing for your captors, and now that I'm one of the good guys, you've lost your initial thrill. Am I getting close?"

My face scrunches in disgust. "That was a hit below the belt, and you know it."

Squeezing his eyes shut, he leans down then rests his forehead against mine. The pain emanating off him breaks me.

"I'm sorry," he chokes out. "You're right, Little Bird. I just...."

"I know," I murmur, hating how easily I accept his apology. "I can't be away from you. You don't know how much it killed me to walk down those steps only to see you beside someone else." My eyes well with tears from the memory. "It'll always be you, Dex—"

His mouth is on mine before I can finish my thought, but as soon as my mind catches up with what's happening, the words scatter like raindrops in a hurricane, and I know I could drown in his kiss. Fisting the lapels on his tux, I tug him closer, but it isn't enough to satisfy the need pulsing through me. I fumble with his slacks in search of connecting with him in a way I've been missing ever since he rescued me from Burlone's prison. He knows me well enough to see right through my scrambling and hoists my red dress up to my waist. The cool air kisses my bare thighs, amplifying my need to have him closer.

"Anxious, Little Bird?" he teases.

"You know me. Always one to take advantage of an opportunity when I see it."

With a deep laugh, he unbuttons his pants while diving in for another kiss. Maybe one day, we'll reach a point in our relationship where we can have sex on a bed like a normal couple. But for now, it appears we're still stuck in moments that involve stolen kisses with a side of sponta- neous dry humping.

Or...not so dry, I note as my hand slides down his chest before gripping his erection. The heat from it scorches my palm, and I can't help but give it a deliberate squeeze in appreciation.

"Careful, Little Bird," Dex grunts while simultaneously thrusting into my hand. "I've been craving you for way too long—"

"And now you have me," I quip. "The question is…are you up for the challenge of getting me off before someone from the party catches us with our pants down?"

His rumble of laughter makes my heart sing.

"Always so bossy, Little Bird," he teases with a look of amused adoration. Bending down, his fingers dig into my bare thighs then he enters me with one swift thrust.

"Shiiiiit," I moan under my breath, squeezing my eyes shut and counting my lucky stars that he's finally inside of me.

"Like that, Little Bird?"

"Mmmhmmm," I hum before rolling my hips into him. His hands tighten along my thighs as he holds me in place, and the orgasm that I know is imminent builds until I'm ready to—

"Shit! I'm so sorry! I'll just—"

Our necks snap in unison toward the open doorway that's currently framing a very surprised Ace. Her deer in the headlights look would be comical if she hadn't just literally caught Dex with his pants down and me with my dress shoved above my waist. Covering her eyes with her hands, she steps back before rocking forward, then back again like the most indecisive person I've ever seen.

"Shit. Sorry. I just, uh—" She lets out a gust of air before gathering her thoughts and stating, "Dex. A guy's looking for you. Dominic…Castello? I think? I told him I'd find you and uh…deliver the message. So. Yeah. That's what I'm doing. I'll just uh. I'll just go now." Turning on her heel, Ace steps out before using her hand as a shield and looking at the door. Once she finds the object she'd been searching for, she grabs the handle and closes the solid piece of oak with a little more force than necessary.

Carefully, Dex sets me back onto the ground and makes sure my dress is situated. After inspecting me from head to toe and deciding I must look presentable enough, he tucks himself back into his slacks then zips them back up.

The silence in the room is unbearable. But I don't know what to say. The repercussions for what we just did could be catastrophic. My brother's girlfriend just caught one of his soldiers breaking a very specific order. If she tells Kingston what she saw…. My entire body starts to tremble with anxiety before I cover my mouth and stare at Dex.

"If she says anything—"

"She won't." He doesn't look very confident. And I don't blame him. Sure, she's my best friend, and we would do anything for each other. But I've seen the way she looks at Kingston. And when you find a love like that, a love like the one I share with Dex, you'd sacrifice anything to have it, and you wouldn't let anything come between it, either. Even your best friend.

"Dex," I start, my voice cracking as I whisper his name.

His big, brooding body cages me against the wall before he tucks a strand of hair behind my ear. "She won't, Little Bird. Everything is going to be okay, but I need to get out there before anyone else comes looking and finds us in here. Understand?"

I give him a jerky nod.

"Good. I love you, okay? No matter what happens, I don't regret what we just did. Understand?"

My throat feels like sandpaper as I try to swallow back my tears, but one still manages to slip past my shaky barrier. Swiping his thumb along my cheek, he catches the moisture then kisses my forehead.

"I gotta go."

"Go," I order. "I'll be okay."

"You sure?"

"Yeah." I nod, unsure if I'm trying to convince him or myself. "Yeah, I'll be fine. We shouldn't walk out of here together anyway, right?"

I can feel his eyes take in every inch of my face before he finally gives in and steps away. "I'll come find you later."

Then he's gone.

But the ghost of his touch still lingers on my skin, making me miss him more than ever. Especially when I'm unsure if it'll be the last time I feel him.

CHAPTER THIRTY-EIGHT

DEX

*M*y Little Bird didn't mention it, but I still rub my thumb along my mouth in case any of her deep red lipstick might've found its way onto my skin during our...*encounter.* I glance down at my thumb and confirm it's crimson free before rounding the corner to the gathering that feels a hell of a lot more like a funeral after I was caught screwing the princess of the Romano family.

Bianca spots me from across the room, waggling her fingers back and forth flirtatiously while balancing a glass of dark red wine in her other hand. I don't bother to return the gesture as I continue scanning the premises for her brother, Dominic Castello.

What the hell is he doing here, anyway?

And what the hell was Kingston thinking by allowing him to enter in the first place?

When I catch Ace staring at me beside Kingston, her face turns pink, and she becomes very invested in her hors d'oeuvres. I'll be needing to chat with her too. I just pray that she doesn't say anything to Kingston before we've had a chance to talk about what she witnessed. If she does, it'll be my head that rolls.

Tugging on the white collar of my shirt, I continue my perusal of the premises. For a guy that was supposedly looking for me, he's pretty damn absent right now. When a soft hand squeezes my ass, I glance over my shoulder before gritting my teeth.

"Little busy, Bianca."

"I can see that," she notes. "Are you looking for someone?"

"Your brother," I answer. "I thought you said he wasn't here?"

Her pouty mouth forms a frown. "Apparently, he changed his mind. He's out on the balcony. You should join him."

I hold her beady gaze for a split second before heeding her advice and heading to the balcony off the side of the estate. It's getting colder, but I don't bother to grab a coat as I step into the brisk air. Sticking my hands into my front pockets, my shoulders bunch up around my ears.

Sure enough, there's Dominic Castello. The bastard who gave Burlone Regina's picture while simultaneously plastering a target on her back.

And he's going to die for it. But first, I need to know what the hell he wants to talk about.

"Hello, Dex," he greets me, balancing a cigarette between his fingers.

Stalking closer, I reply coolly, "Hello, Dominic."

"Congrats on the whole"—he waves his hand through the air—"Romano family thing."

I almost snort. "Thanks."

201

"Good catch, by the way."

My eyes narrow for a split second before I smooth out my features. "For?"

"For finding out your fearless leader was a rat. I heard you were the one who suspected it then brought the issue to Kingston in hopes of finding a...*solution* fit for a snitch."

He means putting a bullet in Burlone's skull without the entire Allegretti family hunting me down afterward.

After inhaling some more nicotine through his cigarette, he asks, "Tell me, do you know what they did with the girls?"

"Girls?"

"You know...the fruit Burlone had acquired for the tournament. Where are they?"

I cock my head while fully understanding that he's prying for something. I'm just not sure what it is. "Why do you want to know?"

"I have a.... Well, let's call him an associate, shall we? He's looking for one in particular."

I do the math in my head, crossing off names and faces in search of which girl he might be especially interested in. Other than Regina and Q, the rest of the girls were taken in by the Feds before likely being returned to their families in shitty condition. If his associate was looking for any of them, he wouldn't have to look very hard to locate their whereabouts. But they were merely apples. A dime a dozen. It would be easier to simply pick a different apple than it would be to find the same one alone and unsuspecting.

And if he spoke to any man at the gathering, he'd know that Regina is here. Which means he's talking about Q. The question is, what does he want with her?

"Which one?" I ask, pretending to be oblivious.

Shrugging, he replies, "Blonde. Pretty. A virgin."

Q.

"She's dead," I offer blandly, about to turn on my heel and end this ludicrous conversation.

He stops me with a condescending tsk that grates on my nerves. "I don't believe you. Where is she?"

"What does your associate want with her?" I counter.

"He didn't say. But he did mention that you'd be generously compensated for any information you have in regards to her whereabouts."

"I don't need money."

He laughs. "No. I don't believe that money has ever really made you tick, now, has it? But power and respect?"

I stay silent.

"Yeah, I think both of those definitely hold more value to you. Especially when you've had so little for your entire life."

"And your associate could provide these things?" I inquire, digging for information that might narrow down who his associate might be.

With a mischievous grin, he answers, "I think you'd be surprised."

"Then why is he not speaking with me directly instead of sending someone else to do his bidding?"

Something isn't adding up, but I can't quite put my finger on what it is. Did they find out that she outed herself as an FBI agent even though it was a bunch of bullshit? And why wouldn't they just come to me directly instead of sending a dumbass like Dominic to retrieve answers? It doesn't make sense...unless whoever is asking questions wants to keep his identity a secret.

My mind continues to churn with possibilities as Dominic remarks, "I don't ask questions, Dex. I only follow orders and pocket the cash that follows."

"What's so special about this girl?"

He shrugs. "Like I said, I don't ask questions. But I will say that he's very confident you'll deliver, and if you do, then he'll be happy to help set things right."

Scratching the scruff along my jaw, I look out at the gorgeous landscape below while contemplating the situation that just presented itself.

After a few tense seconds, I ask, "What kind of things?"

"The Allegrettis are in turmoil right now, Dex. They need a leader. They need someone to step up and take over. You're the perfect candidate, don't you think? Someone who's spent years learning the ins and outs of Burlone's business?" He shrugs, bringing the cigarette to his lips, but before taking another hit, he adds, "And who knows? Maybe the Romanos could use some new management, as well."

I shake my head as every instinct in my body tells me to pull out my gun and end Dominic where he stands. "And you think your associate can deliver on something that big?"

Adam's apple bobbing, he releases more smoke he'd been holding hostage in his lungs. "As I said, I think you'd be surprised."

"When can I meet him?"

He scoffs, rolling his eyes at my ludicrous request. "That's not possible."

"If he wants her enough—"

"It's not an option," Dominic reiterates, growing frustrated. "I'll be the go-between for the foreseeable future, and that's not negotiable."

Interesting.

"Will you be sticking around to enjoy the festivities?" I ask.

"Would you suggest that it would be in my best interest to do so?"

Probably not, I want to reply, but I keep my sarcasm in check before responding, "Yeah. I think it could potentially be beneficial for you. Give me a minute to do some digging. I'll be back in a few."

"Then it looks like I'll be sticking around for a bit." He turns around and rests his elbows on the dark railing before taking another puff from his cigarette that's basically a nub. I watch a bit of ash fall from the tip of it then head inside.

CHAPTER THIRTY-NINE

DEX

The party is still in full swing, but I don't acknowledge anyone as I search for Kingston. When I find him speaking with Matteo Moretti, my steps falter for an instant. Then I approach them.

Clearing my throat, I mutter, "Hey, Boss?"

Kingston turns his attention from Matteo to me. "Yes?"

"We need to talk."

Sensing my urgency, he excuses himself from Matteo and follows me as I search for some privacy.

"Come in here," Kingston orders as we pass the door Regina and I had sex in.

My jaw tightens, but I do as I'm told, praying the scent of sex has dissipated.

Once the door is closed behind us, Kingston demands, "What is it?"

"I received an interesting proposition tonight."

He quirks his brow. "And?"

"And I think you might be interested to know that it

involved me becoming the new head of the Allegretti and the Romano families," I quip, nearly rolling my eyes at the ridiculousness of it all.

Gaze narrowing in suspicion, he probes, "And who made this proposition?"

"Dominic Castello. Which reminds me, why the hell was Dominic Castello, or even Matteo fucking Moretti, invited tonight?"

He grins. "There's a saying, Dex. Keep your friends close and your enemies closer. We had a statement to make this evening, and I think it came across perfectly. I think the real question is, how would Dominic Castello deliver the Allegretti and the Romano families into your care? And what would he want enough to put himself at that much risk?"

"That's the interesting part," I divulge. "He's working for someone but wouldn't tell me who. Whoever it is, he wants Q."

Kingston's eyes open wide in surprise. "What the hell does he want with Q?"

I shrug. "No idea. Maybe someone found out that she outed herself as a Fed, and they want to deliver their own form of retribution."

"I told the men I'd take care of it."

"Yeah, but there wasn't a body in the newspapers to corroborate your story." Rubbing my face in frustration, I offer, "Maybe someone saw her alive? I don't really know, but he's risking a hell of a lot to get her. She's still with Diece, right?"

With a nod, a curious Kingston inspects the situation from all sides before asking, "I think Dominic and I need to have a little chat. Is he still here?"

"I told him to wait on the balcony."

"Why the hell would he do that?"

"Because I gave him the impression that I was interested in his proposition."

His face looks like it's been made from stone as he assesses me closely. "Are you?"

"Do you really even need to ask that?" I return. "I'm your man, Kingston. I've already proven that, haven't I?"

His expression stays calm and indifferent, but I can see the wheels turning inside his head as he weighs my comment, searching for its validity. After a few moments, he finally throws me a bone.

"If Dominic has a connection with whoever's been screwing with the Romanos, then yes. You've proven your loyalty."

Again, I want to point out. It's as if returning his sister and saving his ass did nothing to clear my name.

Biting my tongue, I go a different route and ask, "What do you mean?"

"Since my father died, I've had a suspicion that there's a rat in the organization. We found the first one, but...."

"But something still felt off," I finish for him. "And you were using me to flesh out any more."

It makes sense. I'm the black sheep in the Romano family. If someone was looking for an ally to bring the Romanos down, I'd be the perfect candidate. Apparently, Kingston surmised the same thing.

He doesn't confirm my suspicion. "Let's hope that Dominic holds the answers."

"If you approach Dominic, and we let him walk out of here, he'll tip off whoever he's working with that I can't be trusted, and we'll lose the only lead we have."

"Who said Dominic is walking out of here?" Kingston returns.

My eyes widen in surprise. "You want to put him in the ground too?"

"The sooner our enemies learn the consequences of messing with the Romanos, the sooner they'll figure out it's a terrible idea, and I'll be able to focus on more important shit."

I don't miss the way he says *our* enemies as he pulls out his phone and sends a quick text to someone.

Shifting my weight between my feet, I offer, "I should probably tell you that Dominic Castello is the one who gave Burlone Regina's picture."

"I know," he admits, glancing up at me from his phone before putting it back into his pocket.

"What?"

"It's another reason why he won't be walking out of here tonight."

I'm so damn sick of all these secrets that I want to rip my hair out. "Were you planning on gutting him before he approached me? And will there be any major consequences of his death?"

With a dark laugh, he explains, "My enemies need to understand that I'm not soft. And I won't let them get away with the shit my dad did. As far as consequences for Dominic's death"––he grins, showcasing that he really is batshit crazy––"let's go find out."

A soft knock on the door grabs our attention a few seconds later.

"Got your text," Stefan tells Kingston as he enters the room. "You sure that it's a good idea to do this with guests in the house?"

"I don't see a better time in the foreseeable future, so we'll deal with the hand we've been dealt. Let's try to keep this discreet, though. Once we get him to the shed, we'll get him to sing like a songbird. But for now, we need to keep him quiet until we have some privacy. Dex, do you think you can convince him to follow you outside?"

I nod. "Yeah. I'll see what I can do."

"Good. We'll meet you around back." Kingston stops near the door before turning back to me and stating, "And if it wasn't clear, this is me trusting you. Don't screw it up."

Then he leaves.

CHAPTER FORTY

DEX

I step out of the room a few minutes later, nearly toppling over Regina as she passes by.

"Shit! You okay?" I ask, gripping her shoulders to keep her steady.

She nods before glancing left and right to confirm we're relatively alone. When she finds the hall empty, she whispers sharply, "Where have you been? I've been freaking out! You went missing, then my brother disappeared, and I thought—"

"Shh...," I croon, rubbing my hands up and down her bare skin. "It's fine. Ace didn't say anything." *Yet.* "But I have somewhere I need to be. I'll come find you later, okay?"

Breathing a sigh of relief, she nods. "Okay. I'll uh, I'll see you later. Be careful."

I grin. "Always, Little Bird."

Then I step around her and saunter toward the balcony, praying Dominic's still out there. His silhouette is still where I left him. As I open the door, I approach with a casual swagger to put his rigid posture at ease. "I have the information you're looking for."

"Already?"

"You'd be surprised what a guy like me can turn up when I'm given the right motivation."

His eyes light up, and his triumph tugs at his lips. "Great! Where is it?"

"Follow me." Tilting my head toward the exit, I wait for him to push off from the railing and accompany me to the shed.

Spine straightening, he questions, "Why can't you give the information to me right now?"

I drop my voice low. "This might seem like a relatively private location, but I'm not stupid. Follow me, or I'm out. You decide." Sauntering back to the exit, I don't wait to see if he joins me because I already know he will. Weaving between people, I step through the front door then down a small set of stairs before rounding the side of the house. The sound of footsteps follows me, confirming my assumption that Dominic's a good little dog who knows how to obey orders.

Once we're out of sight from the regular party-goers, I pull him to the side.

"What are you doing?" he asks, his gaze darting around the grassy yard like a deer during hunting season.

I lift my chin toward the shed tucked to the side of the estate. "She's in there."

Jaw dropping, he asks, "She's...she's in there?"

"Yeah. Head inside. I'll pull a car around, and we'll take her wherever you want."

"B-but I have no idea where we'd need to take her yet. I—"

"Do you want her or not?" I grit out, feigning frustration.

"Well, yeah, but—"

"Then get your ass in there. She's already drugged out of her mind. I guarantee she won't make a fuss, and you'll have plenty of privacy if you want to spend a few minutes to sample anything…." I let my voice trail off, giving him a chance to let his imagination run wild. I've dealt with scum like him in the past. For too long, if I'm being honest, and I know that it doesn't take much for their judgment to be clouded when given the opportunity to sample the fruit beforehand.

Sick bastard.

"Oh. Uh…sure. I'll just…go check then." He walks toward the shed door before glancing over his shoulder. He's close to backing out as his self-preservation instinct starts to rear its ugly head, so I march toward him and seethe, "Don't forget to hold up your end of the deal, Castello. I'm not putting my neck on the line for an asshole who can't deliver. We clear?"

His eyes darken. "Yeah."

"Good. I'll go get the car. The door is unlocked. I checked on her a few minutes ago and left it unlatched for you. Like I said, she isn't going anywhere, but stay quiet. I'll be back in ten."

Then I storm off, banking that he'll do as I ask.

Once I'm out of sight, I count to ten before heading back to the shed. When I step inside, Stefan has his hand over Dominic's mouth and is wrestling him into the chair that sits in the center of the empty room. I've never been here before, but it looks almost exactly as I would expect it to. The floor is gray cement with a slight slant that leads to a drain in the center of the room. It's conveniently located beneath the chair to help clean up any messes that inevitably happen here. Along the back wall, there's a locked cabinet that I assume holds a variety of instruments needed for pulling information out of any of Kingston's guests. The walls are metal too, made for easy cleaning with a power hose and a little elbow grease. I can only imagine the scenes they've hidden from public view, but I have a feeling I'll get front row seats tonight.

Stepping toward Stefan as he continues to wrestle with our guest of honor, I pull out my Glock and press it to Dominic's head.

"Stop fighting, or I'll blow your brains out. We just want to chat." The lie is delivered with smooth indifference like I don't care which option he chooses. His eyes practically cross as he looks down the barrel of my gun before nodding his head up and down. After shoving a more compliant Dominic into the metal chair, Stefan cuffs his wrists to the arms and makes sure he can't go anywhere.

Kingston watches with his arms crossed from beside the cabinet. Once he deems Dominic situated, he retrieves a key from his front pocket and opens the gray cabinet.

"Nice to officially meet you, Dominic," Kingston says conversationally while sorting through his stash. "I'm so glad you received our invitation and decided to attend the gathering. Our good friend, Dex, says you had a proposition for him. Care to talk about it?"

Dominic's mouth stays firmly shut, encouraging Kingston to glance over at him before turning his attention back to the cabinet that holds an assortment of instruments used for extracting information. The variety is staggering. Tiny bottles with indistinguishable liquids. A brand new baseball bat. Knives of all shapes and sizes. Hammers. Screws. Hell, there's even a saw in there and a cigar cutter.

"Interesting.... Dex said you were awfully chatty with him, but you seem pretty quiet to me. Dex," he addresses me. "Think you could get this boy talking?"

His question surprises me, especially when he's known for being the king of interrogation. Still, I'm not about to point that out to him, and who knows? This might be another test.

"Sure thing, Boss."

I don't bother to grab any of Kingston's nifty tools. Instead, I raise my closed fist, cock my arm back, and nail him square in the nose. The crunch confirms it's broken, causing a smile to stretch across my face. Dominic's head snaps back as blood flows like a faucet over his lips and down his chin, staining his once white button-up shirt.

"What the hell?!" he screams.

"You're surprised?" I laugh. "I'm a Romano, Dominic. Bribery won't be changing that. Now, we can do this the easy way, and you can start talking, or we can do this the hard way, and I can have Kingston show me how handy his little cabinet is. What do you say?"

He shakes his head, so I hit him again.

And again.

And again.

My fists ache, and my knuckles swell from the abuse, but it doesn't stop me from taking another swing. Crimson-stained saliva spews from his mouth before his head rolls forward, and his chin drops to his chest.

"F-fine," Dominic grunts in defeat. "Fine. J-just...stop."

"I stop when you start talking," I tell him.

"W-what…." He groans in pain. "What do you want to know?"

"We want to know who you're working for."

His eyes roll back in his head, but Stefan steps closer and squeezes his neck in warning. "Don't pass out, Dominic. You won't like how we wake you up."

Heavy lids snapping open, Dominic tries to concentrate and answer the question. "I've never met him. I-I don't know his name. He, uh…he reached out to me. Offered a shitton of money. All I had to do was contact Sei or Dex."

"Sei's in custody," I correct him.

Shaking his head back and forth, Dominic argues, "No. He wasn't picked up with everyone else. Thank God I had the flu and couldn't attend, either, or I'd have been screwed like the rest of them. Then again, I think that's why the guy contacted me in the first place. He knew we ran in the same circle. That I could reach you."

"Stefan," Kingston barks. "Ask Leo to confirm Sei's whereabouts." Turning to Dominic, he continues his interrogation. "What did he want you to contact Dex about?"

"The blonde who slipped through the cracks."

"He wants her?"

Dominic's head drops forward in an exaggerated nod.

"What does your boss want with the girl?" Kingston growls.

"H-he didn't say."

"And you've never met him?"

His attempt at shaking his head is quickly followed by

a grimace, confirming my suspicion that I gifted him with a minor concussion. "No."

"Then how the hell did he give you his orders?" I interject.

As a bit of blood-stained saliva dribbles down Dominic's chin, he mumbles, "M-my phone."

"And where is your phone?" Kingston prods.

"F-front pocket."

Kingston raises his chin at me, and I retrieve the cell before tossing it back at him.

"He probably used a burner," I add as Kingston catches the only lead we have.

"Yeah, but Leo might be able to give us a location by tracking the cell towers he used to contact Dominic," Kingston counters. "And who knows? The bastard might still have the phone on him."

"If they communicated through text, we might be able to convince him to meet up, too," I return.

Turning back to our almost unconscious friend, Kingston asks, "What's your passcode?"

Deep wrinkles line Dominic's forehead, showcasing his pain, but he doesn't respond.

"Now," Kingston orders in a frigid tone.

"4-3-6...." With another groan, he squeezes his eyes shut and repeats, "4-3-6-5-2-0."

"Stefan!" Kingston calls out. "Take this to Leo. See what he can find."

Rushing to Kingston, Stefan grabs the phone then slips out the door with a quiet click.

After we're blanketed in silence, I ask, "What do you want me to do with him?" My gaze shoots to a barely conscious Dominic.

"Leave him here for now. We might need some more info before he pays for revealing Regina's identity. And good work. I can see why Burlone used you for his muscle."

I laugh. "See? I come in handy on occasion."

"Apparently, you do. Now, let's get out of here."

CHAPTER FORTY-ONE

DEX

*T*he party is finally quieting down when we step back into the Romano estate. Only a few stragglers are left, but I can barely contain my annoyance as one of them approaches.

"Hey," Bianca purrs.

"Party's over. Go home."

Hand gliding from my shoulder, then down to my ass, she gives it a firm squeeze. "Or it could just be starting."

My fingers wrap around her delicate wrist, wrenching it away with controlled force before I growl, "Not gonna happen. Go home."

"I can't find my brother."

"So? You didn't drive with him, remember? I'm sure he'll turn up."

Her eyes narrow in suspicion, but she's smart enough to keep her over-injected lips shut.

"Go," I push, releasing my hold before I step around her.

I don't bother to see if she listens or not. To be honest,

as long as she leaves me the hell alone, I don't care what she does.

My phone buzzes with a text as I saunter up the stairs to the second floor.

Stefan: Security room. Now.

Taking the steps two at a time, I round the corner then rap my busted-up knuckles against the security room's door.

Tap. Tap. Tap.

"Get in here."

Doing as I'm told, I twist the handle and enter the security room. Leo's sitting behind a heavy metal desk, his fingers tapping against the keys in earnest while Stefan leans against the wall with his phone in his hand.

"Hey. We're just waiting on Kingston," Stefan explains before turning his attention back to whatever's on his iPhone. Sucking my lower lip into my mouth, I observe the room I've never been privy to enter before tonight.

Apparently, Kingston wasn't kidding about earning his trust.

The walls are painted a dark gray and are lined with monitors showcasing different parts of the house. My gut tightens when my attention falls on a screen that frames a view of the room Regina and I had sex in.

If Kingston sees that footage….

A creak sounds behind me, and I glance over my shoulder to see Kingston.

"Hey, Boss," Leo greets him without bothering to look up from his computer screen.

"Hey. Any luck?"

Nodding, Leo's fingers continue tapping against the desktop in front of him. "Yeah. The dumbass didn't delete any of his messages, and we were able to track it to a quarter-mile radius in The District."

"The District?" Kingston repeats, unable to hide his surprise. Striding closer, he leans over Leo's shoulder to inspect a map of the city more closely.

"Yeah."

"Who the hell do we know that's around The District?"

Silence follows Kingston's question before he turns and stares at me point-blank. "Do you know anyone around there? Anyone who has a problem with the Romanos? Anyone who Burlone used to deal with? Anyone?"

My mind churning for options, I slip my hands into my slack pockets before shaking my head. "Nah, Boss. That's cop territory. Some of Burlone's associates might've enjoyed living on the edge, but no one was suicidal enough to share a backyard with the Feds."

After another beat of silence, Kingston barks, "Leo, call Diece. I want to hear his thoughts."

A speaker crackles a few seconds later, followed by the clear sound of a dial tone.

Ring. Ring. Ring.

"Hello?" a voice answers.

"Hey, D. It's Leo. We have you on speakerphone," Leo explains in a crisp, clear voice.

"Hey, guys," he acknowledges. "Who's all there?"

"Kingston, Stefan, Dex, and me," Leo explains.

"Okay. What's up?"

Clearing his throat, Kingston answers, "How's Q?"

There's a slight pause.

"She's uh…she's fine," D murmurs.

"Has she mentioned anything about her past?"

A drawn-out pause, longer this time, is Kingston's only answer before D clears his throat. "No. Why?"

"Because we had a visitor asking about her," Kingston divulges. "Do you think she's capable of hiding something?"

Another pause.

"I dunno, Kingston. I think she's pretty messed up after everything that happened."

"I need you to bring her back here. We need to chat."

"I don't think that's a good idea."

"And I don't give a shit," Kingston counters. "Someone contacted Dominic Castello and asked him to reach out to Dex to see where the pretty blonde virgin ended up."

"Why the hell would someone be asking about Q?" he growls low in his throat. The threat is clear in his voice, and it's easy to hear that he doesn't like anyone sniffing around her.

"That's what we want to know."

"Do you think the guy who contacted Dex might be…." Diece's voice trails off.

"Do I think he might be the same guy trying to screw over the Romanos?" Kingston finishes for him, show-casing his trust for the thousandth time in one night. "I don't know. They might be related. They might not be."

"It's possible," I interject. All eyes turn to me as I explain. "Dominic said the guy was willing to give me the Romano family as a gift for my loyalty. Sounded to me like he was willing to kill two birds with one stone, ya know what I mean?"

A cold Kingston nods but doesn't comment on it.

Instead, he gets to the point of his phone call. "D, do we know any enemies in The District? Leo tracked Dominic's conversation with whoever his contact is. It led us there."

"But that's Fed territory."

"It is...," Kingston confirms.

A longer pause is drawn out before Diece mutters, "We only know one Fed."

Kingston's mouth forms a long, thin line as he breathes, "Yeah."

"Why would Jack double-cross us? Why would he be looking for Q in the first place?"

"I don't know," Kingston answers, shaking his head. "But I also don't know who else would be interested in the Romanos or any of the girls who were initially taken by Burlone who happen to work in The District. Do you?"

"Shit."

"Who's Jack?" I interrupt, needing to catch up when I'm aware I'm missing a very large piece of the puzzle.

Kingston eyes me warily before explaining, "Jack is the Fed who gave us the fabricated documents that framed Burlone as a snitch. He's also the guy you contacted with the location of Burlone's body."

"So, he double-crossed us?"

"Either that or he works with someone who is double-crossing him," Stefan chimes in with his two cents.

Kingston waves him off. "Regardless, I think it's time we bring him in for a little chat."

"And if he doesn't feel like talking?" Dominic is one thing, but messing with a Fed is an entirely different matter.

With an arrogant smirk from Kingston, followed by a dark chuckle from Diece through the speaker, Kingston divulges, "That won't be a problem. Bring him in, Dex. Leo, will you get you his address. And D?"

"Yeah?"

"I wasn't kidding about having a little chat with Q too. Understand?"

There's a heavy silence that follows, and I'm positive D is debating how he can respectfully disobey his boss's orders before he releases a resigned sigh. "We'll be there as soon as we can."

"Good," Kingston acknowledges. "Let's get to—"

A loud banging noise cuts Kingston off. Tilting my head to the side, I try to place the sound before realizing someone's at the front door. And they sound pissed. Or desperate.

Leo's fingers fly across his keyboard as he comes to the same conclusion. He pulls up a live feed onto one of the largest screens in the room that showcases the front porch of the Romano estate.

With his gaze glued to the image, Kingston breathes, "What the—"

"Who is that?" My attention shifts from Kingston to the stranger at the front door. Blonde hair. Built like a surfer with a stick up his ass. And a dark blue jacket with the letters FBI strewn across the back.

"What's going on?" D's voice vibrates through the speaker. Clearly, he's not amused that he's being left out of the loop. And neither am I.

"Who the hell is that?" I reiterate, growing frustrated.

Tearing his gaze away from the screen, Kingston looks me straight in the eye. "That's Jack Connelly."

CHAPTER FORTY-TWO

JACK

*M*y heart is pounding a million miles a minute as I pound my fist against Kingston fucking Romano's door another time.

"Open up," I mumble under my breath. "Dammit, Kingston! Open up!"

Glancing over my shoulder to confirm I haven't been followed, I find the street empty, but it does nothing to calm my nerves.

The jarring from hitting the door with too much force vibrates down my forearm, but I continue my assault.

"Open the damn door," I growl for what feels like the hundredth time.

With my fist still raised in the air, the solid door opens to reveal Burlone's right-hand man, or ex-right-hand man, along with the Dark King himself.

Tsking, Kingston asks, "What the hell are you doing on my doorstep, Jack?"

I drop my hand to my side and voice a sentence I

never in a million years would've guessed I'd ask a damn mob boss.

Keeping my features smooth, I get straight to the point. "I need your help."

The bastard laughs, and so do his men. "I'm sorry, I must've heard you wrong. Care to repeat that?"

"I said...." I take a deep breath and pray for patience. "I need your help."

"From me?" Kingston grins, though I don't miss the way Dex's hand disappears behind his suit. "Never took you for a funny man, Jack." The bastard is two seconds away from pressing the barrel of a gun to my forehead.

Suspicion spiking, I keep my feet firmly planted where they are, but reply, "Yeah? I guess we'll see how comical you find the situation when I explain what I recently found out, eh?"

"Likewise," he declares, coolly. "And because I'm feeling generous, I'm going to let you dive right in."

I wipe my nose with the back of my hand before glancing over my shoulder. Again.

"Any chance we could do this somewhere more private?"

He stays silent. Watching me. Inspecting me. Analyzing every tiny movement like a fucking lie detector. Because that's exactly what Kingston is. After a few tense seconds, he raises his chin. "Of course. What kind of host would I be if I didn't invite you inside my humble abode?"

He takes a step back, and his men follow suit, giving me plenty of space to enter a place I was sure I'd never step foot in.

Well, not without a warrant, at least. I scoff at the irony before remembering how screwed I really am. While studying the grand staircase leading to the second floor, I can feel Kingston assessing my every move.

"Tell me, Jack, what brings you here on this fine morning?" Kingston inquires. It's almost three in the morning, but I didn't really have a choice to appear this early on my enemy's porch. Not when I knew I couldn't stay home with two unconscious bodies that'd been sent to arrest me.

Kingston motions to a dark leather couch on the left that separates the foyer from a large family room. Dark wood floors are only the beginning of the lavish yet *not* over-the-top decor. Hell, it's almost tasteful.

Conceited bastard.

I take a second to appreciate the furnishings before sitting on the edge of the leather cushion.

"I'm being set up."

There. I said it.

Kingston appears indifferent as he takes a seat across from me on a comfortable two-cushioned sofa. One of his men does the same, but the other, Dex, is out of my sight, though I can feel his presence behind me. My anxiety spikes.

I shouldn't be here.

Leaning forward, Kingston rests his elbows on his knees before asking, "By who? And for what?"

"I-I don't know."

With a condescending tone, Kingston prods, "No theories? Nothing?"

I rub my hand from the top of my forehead and down to my chin, loathing the corner I've been backed into.

"I. Don't. Know."

His jaw stays clenched shut before Kingston brings up a different, and much more tender subject. "Why are you in my house right now, Jack? And I suggest you choose your next words very carefully."

A large hand falls onto my shoulder, pinning me in place, though it's not like I have anywhere else to go. If I did, I wouldn't be here. It seems the Romano family is my only hope.

With a deep breath, I dive right in. "I was at my apartment a few hours ago when a couple of buddies knocked on my door with an arrest warrant. I guess they figured I'd go quietly and didn't think to bring backup."

Kingston's face remains indifferent. "And?"

"And apparently, they found evidence that I was working with Burlone before he died." I laugh dryly at the memory of them pointing their guns in my face when I opened the door to let them inside my apartment. "I asked them what kind of evidence they could possibly have since, ya know, I'm the one who got my hands dirty with you guys in order to catch the bastard. The only thing they were willing to tell me was about the cell phone in my desk that was linked to multiple men in the mob and an email from Burlone saying it was good doing business with me."

The room is quiet. Not a single person moves a muscle as they digest my current predicament before Kingston asks, "Were you doing business with Burlone?"

I shake my head as my blood boils. "Are you serious right now? I would never get into bed with Burlone. He was the lowest scum on this Earth."

"And the other made men you were supposedly in contact with?"

"I'm not a dirty cop," I spit, my frustration finally taking over.

"You made a deal with me, remember?"

"So, because I accepted your deal to take down four pieces of shit in return for a little piece of paper and the biggest shit being wiped from this Earth, you think I'm a dirty cop?"

"You tell me."

I grit my teeth. "I'm here because I'm being framed. I'm here because I have nowhere else to go. And I'm here because you owe me."

Laughing, Kingston refutes, "We had a deal. And that deal is over. I owe you nothing."

"Kingston—"

He raises his hand, and my mouth snaps shut.

"But," he adds, "I might be willing to make another deal if you can prove to me that you aren't the rat who sent Dominic Castello to approach Dex with the opportunity to screw over the Romano family in return for learning the location of one of the girls that went missing the night of the tournament."

"Wait, what?" My mind scrambles to piece together the information he just launched at me like a damn missile.

I don't miss the way his eyes are zeroed in on my face, taking note of every muscle twitch and every damn wrinkle. I must've passed some unknown test because he continues, "I think you heard me just fine, but because I'm feeling generous, I'll give you a more thorough explanation. Earlier this evening, Dominic Castello approached Dex. He was in contact with someone through a burner phone that happened to have sent a text within a quarter-mile of The District. I assume that it happens to be the phone they found in your desk. Whether it was planted there or not remains to be seen. What I want to know is, why would someone in your office want information on a random girl off the street?"

"I-I don't know." My eyes go hazy as I stare at a random sconce on the wall and attempt to sort through all the information that's just been handed to me. Patiently, Kingston and his men wait for me in silence to do exactly that.

Who would want to set me up? Why would someone *want* to set me up? Why would they want information on a random girl who doesn't even have a missing person filled out on her behalf? The only one who even questioned how many girls were at the tournament was—

"No fucking way," I whisper before tugging my attention back to The Dark King across from me. "No fucking way," I repeat, covering my mouth. "I think I know who set me up."

"Tell me."

"Reed. My boss," I spit. "The asshole approached me at my desk after the arrest and wanted to know where the other missing girls were. I told him I didn't know. Then he stormed out of the office. He's been over Burlone's operation for as long as I have. But anytime we were getting close to bringing him in, Burlone would slip through our fingers. It was as if he knew our every move. The only reason we were able to catch him was because you approached me with your idea, and it's not like I was stupid enough to divulge the plan to my superior."

"Which means Burlone was out of the loop for once."

"Yeah," I breathe. "But…it still doesn't make sense. I remember him drilling me time and time again about how terrible Burlone was, and that I'd lose my job if I didn't bring him in. He was putting the whole operation on my shoulders—"

"He wanted to look invested in the case," Kingston murmurs. "If he didn't keep pushing you to bring Burlone in, even if he wanted the opposite, wouldn't that raise more suspicion than him repeating the importance of Burlone's arrest while slipping the guy information to keep him out of prison?"

"Yeah," I admit, feeling sick to my stomach. "I guess it does. But it still doesn't explain why he's so interested in the missing girl."

"Her name is Q." The low rumble of Dex's voice behind me causes my hackles to rise.

Glancing over my shoulder, I nod. "Q. Right."

"We need to figure out why he wants her, and why he chose this moment to frame you," Kingston orders.

I shrug. "I have no idea."

"Then it looks like we have some work to do. Did you kill either of the Feds who came to arrest you?"

"What?" I practically screech in outrage. "Of course not."

"Then how did you escape?"

"There was a...tussle?" I shrug for lack of a better word. "I knocked one out then pinned the other to the ground before cutting off his oxygen supply until he passed out too."

"Could they possibly find any evidence at your place that connects you to the Romano family?"

I shake my head. "No."

"Is there any chance you were followed here?"

Again, I shake my head. "No."

Satisfied, Kingston addresses the man on his right. "Stefan."

"Yeah, Boss?"

"Take Jack to one of the guest rooms. Get him a change of clothes. He'll be staying with us until we can figure out what's going on. Once you're finished, grab Dominic from the shed and take him down to the cellars. He'll be staying with us a bit longer too."

Standing to his full height, Stefan tilts his head to the stairs I'd been inspecting when I first arrived. "Follow me."

CHAPTER FORTY-THREE

DEX

"What do you think?" Kingston's voice is sharp and to the point after Stefan and Jack disappear up the stairs.

"You tell me," I return. "You're the lie detector, right?"

With a smirk, he pushes himself up from the couch on the opposite side of the room and strides toward me. "I want to know your impression of him. I'm afraid my judgment might be a little clouded, given our history."

Scratching the scruff on my jaw, I recount the previous conversation before coming to a conclusion.

"I think he's telling the truth. He looked spooked when we opened the door, and I was checking his pulse when my hand was on his shoulder. It was steady. Elevated," I add. "But steady."

"Okay. I need to call D and make sure he keeps a close eye on Q. They need to be discreet, but they need to get here as soon as possible. I have a feeling too many people are looking for Q right now. If they find her, we'll be screwed by the men I promised that I'd make her disappear from, as well as any cops who will be able to piece together she's been missing, yet was found in the mob's custody."

"Do you need anything from me?"

"Not yet, but I will. Be ready."

"I will be."

With a slap on the back, Kingston disappears down the hall to his office. My stomach grumbles at that same instant, and I realize how damn hungry I am. Rounding the corner to the kitchen, I find Regina pacing back and forth in a pair of sleep shorts and a white tank top while wringing her hands in front of her.

"What are you doing here?" I murmur in a quiet voice before glancing over my shoulder to confirm we're alone.

Her head snaps up as her eyes connect with mine. "I couldn't sleep, so I came down here for a snack or something. Then there was a loud knock at the door. Then you guys came and answered it. And then I heard low voices and--"

"And you were eavesdropping," I finish for her, trying to hide my amusement.

"I wasn't eavesdropping!"

"You were definitely eavesdropping," I conclude before noticing her forehead creased with worry lines. The sight causes me to sober instantly. "You okay, Little Bird?"

Shaking her head, she whispers, "Not really, no."

"What's wrong?" I take a step closer, unable to help myself.

"When I heard Burlone's name…." Her voice catches in her throat before her white teeth bite into her lower lip.

"Shh…." I wrap my arms around her and pull her into

my chest. "He's gone, Little Bird. I won't let anyone ever hurt you again. I promise."

"I know," she whimpers. "I know you won't. I just...I thought this was over. I thought we'd be left alone. That we could just live our lives in peace. But since I've been home, all I've felt is...a sense of unease. Does that make sense?"

"Shh...," I repeat, rubbing my hand up and down her back. "It's going to be okay."

"I don't know if it is. I was naive to our world before I was taken. I mean, I knew my family were technically the bad guys, don't get me wrong, but they weren't really the bad guys to me. They were keeping me locked up in my room under the guise of protecting me, and I always thought they were full of shit. But after everything that's happened, I feel like the blinders have been ripped away from me and that my entire world could come crashing down at any minute. What if I don't have time to be patient? What if we keep waiting for Kingston to give his blessing so that we can live happily ever after, but that day never comes, and we've wasted all this time that we could be together, only for it to never happen? What if—"

My mouth slams down on hers, turning her fears into a soft whimper. Cupping each side of her face with my hands, I angle her head up a little farther, giving myself access to devour her the way I desperately need to. My tongue slides along the seam of her lips before she opens it to grant me entry. Her taste explodes along my taste-buds, dancing along them to give me the perfect combination of sweetness and sass. With a groan, I glide my hand further into her hair until my fingers tangle into her long, dark locks.

"I love you, Dex," she murmurs against my mouth. "I love you so damn much that it hurts."

"I love you too, Little—"

"I gave you one rule," a dark voice rumbles from the hall. I'd recognize it anywhere.

Shiiiiit.

Dropping my hands from Regina's face, I shove her behind me to protect her from the inevitable fallout. It's not like I think Kingston or any of his men would hurt her, but I can't push aside my protective instincts, either. And who knows? This might be the last moment I get to show them to her.

Kingston's pounding footsteps cease once he's a few feet away, but it's easy to see he witnessed me touching someone he specifically told me *not* to touch.

"One rule, Dex. One." He raises his pointer finger toward the ceiling while his face reddens with barely restrained rage.

Regina pleads behind me, "Kingston, please—"

"Not now, Regina," Kingston growls. "Stefan!" he shouts at the top of his lungs.

"It was just a kiss," my Little Bird continues, ignoring her brother's order.

With an icy stare, he looks at the spitfire I fell in love with. "I said, not now."

Footsteps thunder down the stairs before slapping against the hardwood floors in the hallway as Stefan races closer. When he sees Regina cowering behind me and my chest puffed up in defense, his shoulders hunch.

Fists clenched at his sides, he addresses Kingston. "Yeah, Boss?"

"Take Dex out to the shed. It seems he's forgotten what

happens when a soldier disobeys a direct order." Then he storms out, leaving his little sister a sobbing mess in his wake.

Clinging to me, she cries, "No, Stefan. No. Don't take him. Please, you can't do this to him. I love him. I'm begging you. Please—"

Stefan's face loses its color as he takes a deliberate step closer to us. Lifting my finger, I mutter, "I'll go quietly, just...give me a second."

The need to comfort Regina is overwhelming as I give Stefan my back and face her fully.

"Hey, Little Bird." I brush aside some strands of her hair that are sticking to her damp cheeks, but the tears continue to stream down them. "It's okay, baby. It's okay."

"It's not okay," she argues, shaking her head back and forth. "He's going to kill you, Dex. I know what happens in that shed. You can't go in there. Don't let Stefan take you there. Please! I never should've kissed you. I never should've met you. If I hadn't, you'd be safe. You never would've broken Kingston's orders. You never would've—"

"Shh...," I repeat. "It's going to be okay. I don't regret a single moment I've shared with you, Little Bird. Even if I never walk out of that shed, I will never regret what we have. But you need to let Stefan take me, okay? You need to stay strong."

"Dex—"

"I know, baby. I know. I knew what would happen if I disobeyed him, but I don't regret it, and I never will. I need you to promise me that you'll never regret us, either. Do you think you can do that for me, Little Bird? Do you think you can stand strong? That you can face the consequences of our love with a brave face? For me?"

Her lower lip quivers as she shakes her head back and forth.

Lifting her chin with the pad of my finger, I make her look me in the eyes. Damn, she's beautiful. Even when her face is puffy and swollen from crying, she's still the prettiest little bird I've ever laid eyes on. "Be strong, baby. And don't be mad at your brother. He cares about you. He cares about you so damn much that he's willing to rip your heart out to protect you from a guy who doesn't deserve you but stole your heart anyway."

"Dex—"

"Shh...." Carefully, I lean closer and place a close-mouthed kiss onto her trembling lips. "I love you, Little Bird. Be strong. I can handle the consequences of my actions, but I can't handle watching you break. Do you hear me?"

A few more tears rush down her cheeks, dripping off her chin freely as she squeezes her eyes shut.

"Dex...," Stefan murmurs. I can feel his anxiety for giving us this moment, but I don't really give a shit.

"I know," I return before dropping another kiss to Regina's forehead. "I love you, Little Bird. Don't let these repercussions clip your wings, okay? You were made to fly."

Then I drop my arms and walk out the back door toward the shed with my head held high while the girl of my dreams drops to her knees behind me, sobbing for the love we had that's as tragic as Romeo and Juliet's.

CHAPTER FORTY-FOUR

ACE

$\mathcal{I}$ roll onto my side to find Kingston's side of the bed dreadfully empty. With a sigh, I check the time and see it's almost five in the morning, which means he still hasn't slept yet. I went to bed alone after the gathering was officially over, and the guests had cleared out. To say the evening was an interesting experience would be a gross understatement.

Dex had stolen Kingston as I was grabbing another glass of wine, and I haven't seen him since. Squinting at the crack beneath the closed bedroom door, I notice the hallway light is still on. My curiosity finally gets the best of me, and I pad out of our master suite to drag my dark king back to bed.

The sound of quiet sobbing pricks my ears as I reach the bottom of the stairs. My brows furrow in confusion when I realize it's coming from the kitchen. And I'd bet all my money that I know who it belongs to. Digging my teeth into my lower lip, I peek around the corner. With her knees pulled into her chest, a heart-breaking image of Regina greets me.

I knew it.

Cautiously, I approach with my hand outstretched in hopes of not startling her.

"Gigi?" My voice is quiet but sounds louder than a siren in the otherwise silent room.

She doesn't answer me.

"G? You okay? What's wrong?"

My best friend peeks up at me with red-rimmed eyes. And I know something is seriously not okay.

"What's wrong, G?" I press. "Tell me."

"He knows," she whispers. "He knows that Dex didn't follow orders. He took him to the shed, Ace. He took him to the shed. Nothing good happens in the shed. H-he—" She hiccups. "He's going to kill him, Ace. I just know it. And it's all my fault!" Her head falls back into her hands as her back shakes with more sorrow until my heart breaks with it.

"Where's Kingston?" I ask.

"I don't know," she cries.

"Stay here, okay? I'll be right back."

Then I'm racing toward his office, praying I'm not too late.

Grasping the handle, I twist it then push open the door without knocking. Kingston's face is calm and indifferent as he glances up at me, but I know him well enough to see how distraught he is.

"We need to talk," I start.

"I don't really have time right now, Wild Card."

"Then make time."

With a sigh, he sets down his pen then squeezes the back of his neck while eyeing me warily. "What is it?"

"I know he disobeyed your order—"

"Then you know he must be punished for it. I warned him, along with everyone else in this very room, about what would happen if he touched her without my consent."

"I remember," I whisper, approaching him slowly.

"What else does she expect me to do, Ace?" he asks, finally giving me a glimpse of his wariness. "My men need to know that there are repercussions for their actions, and they sure as hell need to know that if I give them an order, they have no choice but to follow it. Family comes first. Always."

"I agree. There should be repercussions for his actions—"

"He disobeyed me!" His frustrations finally burst through the seams as he slams his open palm against the surface of his desk.

"He did," I acknowledge in a soft voice while ignoring his outburst. "And you're right. There should be repercussions for his decision. But tell me this, King." I round the corner and sit in his lap before gently touching the side of his chiseled jaw. "If it were between the family and me, who would you choose?"

"That's not fair," he argues.

"It isn't," I tell him. "But that's exactly what you did to him."

"It's different."

"It really isn't," I repeat, leaning forward and pressing my mouth to his in a quick kiss. "He's a Romano, Kingston. And I can guarantee that if it were any other order, he'd follow it to a T, but you demanded an impossible task, and you know it."

"I have an obligation to this family—"

"And he has an obligation to her," I argue. "He loves her, Kingston. He's been loyal to this family with every other task you've thrown at him. I'd like to think that, if the roles were reversed, you'd do the same for me. That our love would be all-consuming and that you'd have no choice but to be there for me the same way Dex has been there for Gigi."

"Then what would you have me do, Wild Card? If I let him off the hook, then my men will think I'm weak. They'll think I'm picking favorites. They won't take my orders seriously. They'll question my judgment. And they sure as hell won't respect me or my position as the head of this family. You know I can't let that happen."

The worry lines around his eyes nearly break me because I know he doesn't show them to anyone else. Ever. But he's showing them to me. Leaning forward, I press another kiss to his mouth, lingering a little longer this time. When I pull away, his eyes are closed, but his lips part to release a slow sigh like he can finally breathe for just a second.

Satisfied, I continue, "You're right. You need to remind your men that there are consequences of disobeying an order. But you also need to show your sister that you love her. And you need to show your best friend's brother a little grace when, if the roles were reversed, I'd like to think you'd make the same mistake for me."

His gaze snaps to mine before his fingers find the back of my neck, digging into my flesh as he pulls me forward and punishes me with a forceful kiss that makes my toes curl.

"I'd kill for you, Ace. And you know I'd die for you too."

"And so would Dex. Demand his loyalty, but understand that there's only one person who will ever come before the Romano family. Besides, wouldn't you want that for your sister? Someone who would kill for her but die for her too?"

His silence is answer enough, but I wait for him to come to the same conclusion that I know he will if I give him a little time.

After a few minutes, he mutters, "Take Regina to her room. And inform her that her punishment will be witnessing me administer Dex's."

"Are you sure?"

"Don't push me, Ace," he snaps.

With a gulp, I lick my lips then nod. "Okay."

CHAPTER FORTY-FIVE

DEX

A bead of sweat slides down my back as the seconds tick by. I don't know how long I've been sitting in this damn metal chair, but my ass is starting to go numb.

Gingerly, I shift in my seat before glancing toward the foreboding cabinet in the corner near the back wall. Stefan leans his shoulder against it, finally ending his incessant pacing as he pulls out his phone to check the time. Apparently, I'm not the only one who feels anxious.

"What time is it?" I mutter, breaking the heavy silence.

"Eight."

Doing the math, I realize I've been sitting here for almost four hours, and I haven't slept in almost thirty-six.

"Did he say when he was coming?" I ask.

"Nope."

"Have you heard from him?"

"Nope," he repeats.

After another beat of silence, Stefan lets out a groan

before rubbing the palm of his hand across his face. "Why'd you do it, man? I told you to be patient."

"I know. But keeping my distance from her was...." I pause to search for a word that accurately describes how unbearable it is. Then I realize there isn't one that's powerful enough to do my feelings justice. With a shrug, I continue, "It was impossible, man. It was like Kingston told me to stop breathing. I could only do it for so long before instinct would take over, and I'd lose the battle."

She's my air.

With a somber nod, his eyes glaze over, and he stares into the distance as if processing my remark.

Convinced he's going to drop it, I replay my last moments with Regina, wishing I'd savored her kiss a little longer. That I'd threaded my fingers through her silky hair one more time. That I'd told her I'd loved her from the moment I saw her caged away in that basement.

"Do you regret it?" Stefan inquires, pulling me from my reverie.

I shake my head. "I regret a lot of shit in my life, but I'll never regret a single minute that I shared with her."

"Even if King follows through with your punishment?" he presses.

"My only regret will be that I tried to keep my distance from her in the first place. If I knew my days were numbered, I would've spent every single one of them with her in my arms."

"I'm sorry, Dex."

"Don't be. If our roles were swapped, I'd be following orders too. Family first. Always." I snort, shocking myself that I could find any of this messed up situation amusing. "Well, except when Regina's in the mix."

Laughing, he points out, "Yeah, I'm not sure that'll get you a free pass even if she's Kingston's little sister."

"I'm not asking for a free pass," I admit. "I know the screwed up situation I put Kingston in. If he doesn't follow through with his threat, he'll lose respect from every single one of his men. And if that happens, the family falls apart, and the Romano name is spoiled. He'd be a fool to let me get away with touching Regina."

"And he isn't a fool."

My throat feels like sandpaper as I mutter, "No. He definitely isn't."

* * *

THE LOUD SCRAPING of metal on metal rouses me from my restless sleep. Head snapping up, I look over my shoulder at the door behind me. Kingston walks through, followed by nearly twenty men who crowd the small shed until they're standing shoulder to shoulder, leaving less than a yard of space between the center of the room where I'm currently chained to a chair, and their stiff bodies.

Curious, I scan each of their faces and place most of them from the gathering the night before. Funny. They were here to welcome me with open arms only a few hours ago. Now, they're here to witness my death. When my gaze lands on Diece, my half-brother, my chest aches.

Sorry, brother, I want to say. *Sorry I screwed up and wasted what little time I had left on this earth instead of reaching out to you sooner.*

His expression is somber. Guarded. Strained. He's here to witness his brother's execution for disobeying orders, and even though our relationship is practically non-existent, it's easy to see the potential of it slipping through our fingers like sand.

The silence is deafening as I wait to hear the click of a gun being cocked. Or maybe it'll be a knife that exacts Kingston's justice. I've heard he enjoys proving a point, but maybe he'll show a bit of mercy to protect his sister's feelings. Or maybe he won't. I can never tell with him.

At least she's not here to witness my demise. I think that would break me more than any torture ever could. Searching for my executioner, I find Kingston near the exit of the shed, waiting patiently for...something. Or at least that's what I assume he's doing. Why else would he be hovering near the door instead of getting this shit over with? Or maybe he likes watching his prisoners squirm. I hold his gaze when he feels my stare and turns to me. That same cool indifference that he's known for is all I get in return.

Rushing footsteps against the gravel path outside grab my attention.

Shit.

Clenching my hands into tight fists, I watch helplessly as Kingston grips Regina's forearm to prevent her from stumbling inside before leaning down to whisper something in her ear.

The tears continue to slide down her cheeks, but she gives him a jerky nod as her gaze finds mine across the room. They hold them for a split second before nearly drowning me in her sorrow. Squeezing her eyes shut, she shrugs out of Kingston's hold then folds her arms across her chest. The pain written across her face hits me harder than my own ever could, though I can tell she's trying to look strong. For me.

And I'm gutted.

I'd give anything to hear what he's said to her, but I'm smart enough to keep my mouth shut.

For now.

With a gentleness I don't expect, he ushers her inside with the palm of his hand resting against her upper back. Once she's settled near the wall by the exit, he parts the crowd like Moses with the Red Sea and addresses his men.

"Gentlemen, do you know why I've invited you here?"

He receives a wave of nods in response, but the silence remains.

Satisfied, he continues. "Early this morning, I found evidence that a man I've trusted, one of *our* men, a man whom I welcomed into the family with open arms," he adds, pausing for effect, "disobeyed a direct order."

I gulp, but hold his stare as it cuts through the crowd like a hot knife through butter. Cocking his head to the side, he scrutinizes me openly.

"It's a shame," he admits, his tone ringing with resigned disappointment. "This same man proved his loyalty only hours before when he delivered a piece of vital information to me. Something he could've easily kept to himself if he chose to do so. Hell, he could've even used it against the Romano family to cause more chaos in an already turbulent time." Raising his hands at his sides, he faces his palms toward the ceiling while motioning to the crowd of soldiers. "The combination has put me in quite the predicament, as I'm sure you can all understand."

Grunts of said understanding rumble throughout the room.

"But before I reach my verdict, it's time for you to all

show him what we do to Romano men who fail to put the family first."

My eyes dart around the room at his ominous words. Each and every one of the men remains in their place but turn their attention from me to my half brother. Weaving between fellow soldiers, he stops a foot in front of me. There's something in his expression that causes my stomach to tighten. I can't quite put my finger on it. Maybe a bit of regret? Disappointment? And mother-fucking stubbornness that makes it clear that whatever's about to happen is going to hurt like a bitch. I watch as he cocks his fist back, and the next thing I know, my head snaps back and a dull ringing pulses in my ears. Opening my eyes wide, I look up at the ceiling as my mind scrambles to register what the hell just happened. I feel like I just got hit with a baseball bat in the jaw. I've been hit before. I've had the shit kicked out of me until I woke up in a pool of my own blood. But that hit? From my own flesh and blood? It hurt. Bad.

"Family first, brother. Always." Diece steps to the side, then another fist connects with my cheekbone, amplifying the ringing in my ears as pain radiates from the fresh hit.

"Family first," the stranger murmurs before another fist slams into my nose. A gush of blood follows it immediately.

Then another hit.

And another.

And another.

Until the room is spinning, and my chin is resting on my heaving chest as I try to shove aside the pain. I can only imagine the mess that I look like. Hell, my eyes are practically swollen shut from having the shit kicked out of me, and I know without a doubt that my nose is broken, and that I likely have a concussion from the beating too.

"Dex." A voice slinks into my consciousness, and I open my eyes to register who it belongs to. *Kingston.* "You came here as nothing but a bastard." I blink my swollen lids to hide my disdain for the term, but he doesn't miss me flinch as the filthy word sinks in.

Bastard.

Stalking closer, he continues, "You were given the opportunity to make a name for yourself that holds respect instead of shame. Do you think you earned it with your actions, despite disobeying a direct order?"

The crowd is silent. Every single eye in the room watches me carefully as they all wait for my response because if Kingston doesn't believe it to be the truth, I'm a goner. The answer gets lodged in my throat, and I force it down with a thick swallow as I search out my Little Bird in the sea of people. When I find her near the exit, I notice she's a mess of emotion from having witnessed my beating. The tears stream down her cheeks steadily as she holds my gaze, and I'd give anything to wipe them away and promise that everything is going to be okay. I'm just not sure that it is. Releasing a slow breath through her pouty mouth, she tries to stay strong while failing miserably.

"Answer me, Dex," Kingston orders, losing his patience.

"I should've spoken up when you first gave your orders. I knew I'd never be able to follow them. I'm your man, Boss. I promise to put this family first in every single circumstance, and I will die for my brothers if the day ever calls for it…with one exception."

"Dex," Regina whispers. I don't hear her murmur my name, but I watch her mouth form it nonetheless.

Kingston grabs my attention by stepping between his sister and myself, effectively cutting off our connection. "I gave you an order—"

"But you required the one thing I couldn't give," I admit. "Do your worst, Kingston. I would expect nothing less from the Dark King, but know that I'll never regret touching your sister, and if you let me out of this room, the only promise I'll be able to make in regards to her is that I'll stop attempting to keep my distance. She's mine. She always will be. That being said, if you show me mercy, you won't regret it. I'm a Romano, and I won't let you down."

"Knife." Kingston spits the word like it's a curse before Stefan rushes forward with a wicked sharp blade cradled in his hand. After placing the handle into Kingston's palm, he retreats into the crowd, and I'm left with the Dark King standing a few feet away from me.

He circles me slowly, but I keep my chin held high and watch his every move with the knowledge that he'll strike at any second. It doesn't help that I'm seeing two of him, though, and his movements only seem to amplify the spinning in my head.

"Men like you are hard to come by, Dex," Kingston acknowledges after a few tense seconds. "And I'm not sure I've finished having you as an ally. For that, I'll let you keep your life, but not without taking something from you first. These hands touched something they weren't meant to touch, so I've decided to give you a daily reminder about what happens when you defy my orders. If you can accept my punishment without making a single sound, I'll let you keep your life...and my sister."

What the hell?

"Do we have a deal?"

I nod, unable to believe he actually offered her to me.

Satisfied with my response, he questions, "Are you right-handed, Dex?"

Again, I nod before his hand squeezes my left wrist, and he orders, "Open your fist and spread your fingers."

Doing as I'm told, I spread my fingers wide and wait for the sharp steel to do their damage.

I'm not disappointed.

The bite of the blade is excruciating as it cuts into the skin on my pinkie, right along the top of my knuckle on the far left finger of my hand. Releasing his hold on my wrist, he grabs my small finger and twists it with precision, popping the joint out of its socket until my finger hangs off the side of my hand at an awkward angle. My bruised jaw tightens, and I dig my teeth into the inside of my cheek until the explosion of blood coats my tastebuds.

Fuuuuuuuck.

I keep my mouth shut, and my swollen eyes glued to my prize, grateful Kingston had bent forward enough to give me a view of her. My Little Bird. Her dainty little hand covers her mouth as she watches her brother saw off my finger. And fuck, it hurts.

Turning pale, I can tell she's about to puke or faint, and I open my mouth to tell Kingston to let her leave the room before remembering I can't make a sound, or he'll accuse me of defying orders a second time. And that will never happen again.

As if she can read my mind, Regina pulls her gaze away from the mess of my left hand. With another deep breath, she focuses on my face, and I try to smooth my features to hide the burning pain radiating from my knuckles, down to my forearm, and up into my shoulder.

Shiiiit, that hurts.

But Kingston is right. I'll never touch his sister ever again without remembering the sacrifice I made to do it, along with the promise I made to him that I'll never put anything above the family ever again. Except her.

Which apparently, is enough for him.

Once I'm positive I'm about to pass out from the excruciating pain, Kingston tosses the finger onto my lap.

"Remember what you saw today, gentlemen. Family first. Always. Next time someone disobeys an order, they lose their hand. Dismissed."

The men file out without any more prodding from their leader, and I'm left with crimson blood dripping from my hand and onto the cold cement floor beneath me.

"Regina," Kingston barks. "You can see him now."

Seconds later, a pair of soft hands frame my face, keeping me from slipping into oblivion.

"Dex? Dex, look at me! Are you okay? I'm so sorry, baby. I'm so sorry that—"

"Shhh...," I whisper, taking in the remnants of yesterday's makeup sliding down her pink cheeks. "It's okay, Little Bird."

Shaking her head, she argues, "It's not okay. Do you have any idea how much it killed me to let him do that to you?" Her voice cracks. "I pushed you into sleeping with me. I pushed you into giving us a chance. This is all my fault, Dex. It's all my fault."

With her arms wrapped around my neck, she sobs. Hard. More than I've ever seen her break down, and that includes the days not so long ago when she was sure she'd be sold as a sex slave. And that's when it hits me. She's sobbing for me. For the pain I just experienced. Hell, the pain I'm still experiencing. She's sobbing for us. And I know without a doubt that she probably offered to take my punishment from me if her brother would let her.

Thankfully, the bastard knew I'd kill him if he accepted.

"Little Bird," I mutter, trying to even out my haggard breathing. "I'm okay."

"You're not okay—"

"I am," I insist through gritted teeth. "But do you wanna know what would make me even more okay?"

She nods.

"If we could take these cuffs off so that we could get the hell out of here."

With the most pathetic smile I've ever seen, she leans forward and places the softest kiss I've ever felt against my lips. Pulling away, Regina searches the room before finding who she's looking for.

"Stefan. Do you have the key?"

"Yeah." Jangling follows his quiet response as he strides closer and unlocks my cuffs. "Sorry I hit you," he apologizes.

"Don't be." I give him a pathetic smile. "I deserved it."

"You look like shit."

My laughter turns into a groan when a cut on my

lower lip splits open. With a grimace, I mutter, "I feel like shit, so that's not exactly surprising. Am I free to go?"

"Yeah. Might wanna put some pressure on your hand, though. You're bleeding everywhere."

My head drops down to inspect the damage. Sure enough, blood flows onto the concrete in a steady stream of droplets.

Rushing toward the cabinet, Regina searches for a few seconds before returning with a small black dish towel. Carefully, she presses it against my wound while my face scrunches up from the pressure.

"Sorry!" she apologizes. "You okay?"

"Fuuu––Fine. I'm fine. Let's get out of here."

I toss my good arm around Regina's neck before she grabs my bad hand and cradles it against her chest, making sure to keep a good amount of pressure with the washcloth to stop the bleeding.

"I think you're going to need stitches or something," she tells me, her face scrunching in pity.

With a dark laugh, I reply, "I think you're right. Do you guys have a doc on speed dial or anything?"

"Yeah. If it were a little more...superficial"—she grimaces at the word—"I'd offer to do it for you, but I don't want to screw it up and cause any more damage."

"You a nurse, baby?" I tease.

A light blush turns her cheeks pink as her gaze drops to the ground. "I've helped out a time or two," she defends herself.

"Does your help come with a"—I breathe deep in an attempt to stave off the pain—"a sexy nurse outfit too?"

With a giant grin stretching across her face, she opens

her mouth to say some smartass remark before it disappears altogether as the sound of a deep voice cuts her off.

"Dex," Kingston addresses me.

Turning around, I reply, "Yeah?"

"Don't screw up again. Understand?"

"I won't."

"Good."

He steps around me to make his escape when I call out, "Hey, King?"

"Yeah?" he answers, turning around grudgingly.

"She mine?"

His gaze shifts to his sister clinging to my side before he gives me a solemn nod. "Yeah, Dex. She's yours, but I suggest you don't screw that up, either."

I laugh, though it's interrupted with another groan. Once I catch my breath, I answer, "Noted."

Then he's gone, and my shoulders sag a little farther, giving Regina a bit more of my weight than I'd ever dare to give her under normal circumstances.

"Let's get the hell out of here."

CHAPTER FORTY-SIX

DEX

*T*he rest of the morning is spent in a blur of stitches and pain killers. Kingston had prepped the doctor about my condition, and as soon as Regina and I entered the house, he got straight to work before ordering me to get some sleep.

He didn't have to put too much effort into persuading me.

With a groan, I roll onto my side and take in the blood-red satin sheets that match the curtains framing the balcony window.

"You sure your brother won't mind that I slept in your room?" I grumble before pushing myself up onto the mattress. I feel like I was run over by a truck. Resting my back against the headboard, I catch Regina with a black pair of glasses balanced on her button nose, and the sight is enough to distract me from my pounding headache. She looks up at me from a chair tucked in the corner of the room, and I can't help but notice the way the light from the window casts a glow on her makeup-free face, showcasing her natural beauty to perfection.

"You held up your end of the bargain by taking his punishment. Now, it's his turn to hold up his end of the deal."

Satisfied with her confidence that I'm not about to be finished off by her brother after everything I went through to get here, I change the subject. "Since when do you wear glasses?"

"Since forever, but they're only for reading. Why?"

"I've never seen you wear them."

"And that surprises you?" she teases, setting aside her book before pushing the glasses off her face until they act as a makeshift headband.

"Kind of. Sometimes I forget how little I know about you."

With the sweetest of smiles, she throws me a bone. "You know everything that matters, but I'm sure we'll both be pleasantly surprised with a few curveballs in the future. Gotta keep each other on our toes, right?"

The sway of her hips distracts me from coming up with a witty remark as she saunters toward the bed.

Once she's within reach, I use my good hand to tug her closer. "Right."

"How are you feeling?" she asks.

My head feels like an elephant sat on it for a few hours, but other than that....

"I'm fine."

"You sure?" Her forehead wrinkles with discomfort, and her mouth purses in distaste as her gaze bounces around my busted up face.

"With a look like that, you're making me question it," I remark dryly.

She laughs, her worry lines disappearing in the blink of an eye. "Sorry. I know guys like you hate pity and stuff, but seriously...your face is making me hurt."

Joining in her contagious laughter, I wrap my right arm around her neck and pull her in for a quick kiss. "Way to stroke my ego. Should I get a brown sack to cover it?"

"That's not what I meant!"

"I'm teasing," I console her. "I'll be fine, Little Bird. Promise."

A loud knock grabs my attention as Regina calls out, "Who is it?"

"It's me," the voice returns. "Stefan."

"Come in."

Turning the handle, he pushes open the door, then grimaces as soon as he sees me. "Dude, your face looks messed up."

I chuckle under my breath while Regina covers her grin at his assessment.

"Gee, thanks," I return sarcastically.

Hovering near the door, Stefan asks, "Do you think you could handle coming down to chat for a bit?"

"Yeah, sure. I'll be down in a few. I just need to grab a change of clothes."

Regina leans into my side. "I already grabbed some for you while you were passed out. You can shower in here if you want."

Face blanching, Stefan mutters, "Aaaand, that's my cue to go. We'll see you downstairs in a few."

"Not like that!" Regina yells at his retreating form, but

it's too late. With bright red cheeks, she slips off the bed and motions to the bathroom door. "Seriously, I didn't mean like—"

"Like we could shower together? Should I be offended by how quickly you turned down that suggestion?"

Grinning down at me, she offers her hand to pull me up, and because I'm a gentleman––and need a giant aspirin––I take it.

"I'm not turning down the opportunity to screw you in the shower, Dex. I just think we might want to wait a few days before we try anything. You know, give yourself a little time to heal."

"I'm fine, Regina," I argue, though my head starts to spin as soon as my feet hit the ground.

"I'm sure you are," she replies with a knowing grin. "But let's give it a few days anyway, okay?"

"No promises."

Guiding me into the bathroom, she turns on the shower then asks, "Do you want me to help you undress?"

"Regina, I'm—"

"I know! You're fine! I get it! I'm just saying…I want to help. Especially after everything you went through for me, I just…I want to take care of you the same way you took care of me, ya know?"

Rolling my tongue between my teeth and cheek, I finally give her a single nod. "But only if you shower with me."

She smirks. "I thought you'd never ask."

Stripping bare is fucking difficult when one hand is practically useless, and I'm so distracted by the spinning room that I miss out on Regina getting naked a few feet away from me. Thankfully, my Little Bird doesn't let me struggle for long before her deft little fingers grab the hem of my shirt and slip off my white undershirt with ease. When her slender body comes into view, I almost swallow my tongue. Tan skin. Hourglass figure. I could get lost inside her for hours if she'd let me. As soon as my mind starts to wander into very dangerous territory, her hands slowly slip down my pecs and abs before landing on the waistband of my boxers. Peeking up at me, she toys with the elastic before bending forward to slide them down my legs.

Which leaves my cock an inch from her face.

"Careful, Little Bird," I warn her. "You told me to take it easy, but you're making that awfully difficult for me."

With a teasing grin, she drops a quick kiss to the tip of me before standing to her full height and guiding me inside the steaming shower. "Like I said, the doctor ordered that you should take it easy for a few days."

"Babe—"

"Keep your hand out of the water. I'll wash your hair for you so that we don't have to redo the bandage yet."

"Someone's bossy," I quip.

"You have no idea." An amused Regina reaches for the shampoo bottle and squirts a nickel-sized amount into the palm of her hand.

"You know, just 'cause I'm missing a finger, and my face is busted up, doesn't mean my dick's broken."

Giggling, she runs her fingers through my hair, massaging my scalp in slow circles while simultaneously pulling a groan from my parted lips.

"My brother's waiting for you downstairs."

"Yeah, and he knows you're mine now."

"But there's a meeting—"

"And it can wait."

"You're stubborn," she points out, encouraging me to tip my head back by pressing the pad of her finger against my chin.

I do as I'm told, withholding another groan of appreciation as the hot water slips from the top of my head and down my spine, the suds swirling down the drain.

"You have no idea," I mimic her words from earlier. "Tell me, do I get a loofah too like the one I offered you before the tournament or...?"

"Are you saying my hospitality isn't as good as yours?" she quips.

"Maybe. I gave you orgasms while under my care. All you've given me are a nasty set of blue balls and a missing finger."

Face turning the color of cherries, she smacks me in the chest. "Dex!"

"I'm kidding!" I laugh, and damn it feels good. "Seriously. He could've taken my life, and it still would've been worth it."

"Don't joke about that," she pouts.

"I'm sorry," I apologize, cupping the side of her face with my right hand while making sure to keep my left one out of the water. "But if I'm being honest, it could've gone a lot worse. Now, I get to keep you. That sounds pretty damn perfect to me."

Her straight, white teeth dig into her lower lip as she deflects my compliment. "You're ridiculous."

"I'm ridiculously in love with you."

With the softest expression, she plants a slow, open-mouthed kiss to my heated skin above my heart then peeks up at me. "I'm ridiculously in love with you too. Promise to keep your hand dry?"

My brows furrow in confusion before looking at my hand that I've kept out of the stream of water since she tugged me into the shower. "Uh…yeah?"

"Promise?" she repeats with a stern look.

I roll my eyes. "I will if you tell me why you're being so bossy."

"I'd hate for you to think my hospitality didn't hold a candle compared to yours even though I did kinda fail on the whole loofah front."

"And?"

Licking her lips, she slips down to her knees. "And apparently, I owe you an orgasm. Just don't tell your doctor and keep your hand out of the water, or I stop."

My gaze darkens. "Always so bossy, Little Bird. Let's see just how hospitable you can be."

CHAPTER FORTY-SEVEN

DEX

"Took you long enough," Stefan calls out as I trudge down the stairs. "We're in here."

Following his voice, I find him, along with Kingston, Diece, and Jack gathered around the kitchen table while playing a hand of Texas Hold 'Em.

"What are you guys doing?" I ask. If I'd have known they only wanted me for a hand of Poker, I would've stayed in the shower a while longer.

"We were waiting for you," Diece answers for me. "Sorry about your face, by the way. I had to make a statement that I stood by Kingston's decision regardless of what it was."

"I figured, and I would've done the same."

"Good." With the toe of his shoe, he pushes out the kitchen chair next to him. "Take a seat."

Plopping down next to him, I watch the rest of the hand play out before Kingston gathers the cards and shuffles them together. Once he's finished, he gets to the point of our impromptu meeting that couldn't wait.

"As you know, Jack has reason to believe his ex-boss was working with Burlone. We don't know to what extent, but I think it'd be beneficial to find out. Unfortunately, he hasn't tried to contact Dominic's cell yet, but that might have something to do with the fact that he was trying to frame Jack with the burner."

"What if we pretend to be Dominic and tell him we have information on Q?" I offer. "Maybe he set up iMessage or something and can read the messages through a computer too?"

My brother goes rigid beside me, and I glance over at him to assess his odd reaction. "If we mention Q, he'll know we have her and might come after her."

"We don't *know* that," I mutter.

"Then why the hell would he be looking for her if he didn't want her?" D seethes. "After the hell she's been through, she deserves to stay hidden, and we owe that to her."

Trying to placate him, I raise my hands in surrender. "If Dominic's contact is Jack's boss, then he already knows Q doesn't work for the FBI, which means he won't believe that we put her in the ground like Kingston had told every single person at the tournament."

"We need to know why she's so important," Jack interjects.

"Agreed," I concur, shifting my gaze back to D, who's growing more and more frustrated by the minute.

Gritting his teeth, he stares darkly back at me. "I've already spoken with her. She doesn't have any answers."

Kingston leans forward, setting aside the cards as he addresses his right-hand man. "Maybe I can help jog her memory."

"I already told you that's a terrible idea."

"And I already told you that she doesn't have a choice. And neither do you."

Growing frustrated, he shakes his head. "She's scared, King. She doesn't respond well to men in general. There's no way she'll be able to answer your questions."

"She seems to respond fine to you," Kingston points out.

With a glare, D mirrors Kingston's position, resting his elbows on the table until the testosterone in the room is suffocating. "It's a bad idea."

"And I don't give a shit. I need to talk to her, D, and that's an order. I need to find out if she remembers anything out of the ordinary from her disappearance. I need to find out who she really is because her story isn't adding up, and if she wants my protection, she needs to be honest with me."

My attention bounces between the two men going head-to-head over an innocent girl who found herself in a screwed up situation that's affecting so much more than a single person. It's affecting the Romano's entire operation, and she just might be the key to solving all of it. Then again, she might be the key to bringing it down too.

My brother doesn't back down under Kingston's scrutiny. Every muscle in his body is tense, ready to spring into action at any second, and I'm afraid I'm seconds away from having to dive between the two of them to keep him in check. Which isn't going to feel good if I rip any stitches.

"She's stronger than you think," I tell D, trying to placate him. "We need to get to the bottom of this."

"Then I stay when you interrogate her," he growls,

staring Kingston down from across the table. "And you promise not to touch a hair on her head. Understand?"

The air pulses with that same violent testosterone as Kingston debates whether or not he should throw out a direct order that could possibly require D's hand as payment for breaking it.

"Fine," Kingston returns coolly. "You can sit in on the interrogation, but if you intervene before she has a chance to explain herself, there will be consequences. We clear?"

Jaw tightening, D spits, "Yeah. We're clear."

"Good. Next order of business. Jack, your face is plastered all over the news. Thankfully, they haven't found any connection between you and the Romano family, but you're officially on house arrest until we figure this shit out. I don't need the Feds knocking on our door with an arrest warrant for you. Understand?"

He nods. "Yeah. If I can help while still staying under the radar, I'm your man."

"Good. It seems that Jack's face being headline news is rocking the boat a bit with Burlone's previous associates, so we'll need to smooth things over. Dex, this is where you come in. I don't care what you have to say; I don't care what you have to do; you will not let any of this messed up situation blow back on us."

"I won't," I promise, my voice ringing with determination.

Sensing my resolution, Kingston nods his approval. "We won't be reaching out to Dominic's contact until I speak with Q, but that doesn't mean I'm not keeping it as an option if we need to move forward with it. Stefan, do you know if Leo has located Sei yet?"

"What?" D shouts, interrupting Stefan from responding.

Again, all eyes turn to him until I can feel the rage rolling off him in waves.

With a sigh, I explain, "Dominic informed us that Sei wasn't captured during the raid."

"But I thought you—"

"Yeah, I know," I reply, growing impatient. "I zip-tied him to a fucking chair and shot enough drugs into his veins to take down a gorilla. I have no idea how he escaped, but he did."

His expression is nothing short of restrained rage boiling beneath the surface as he seethes, "We need to find him."

"He's not our greatest concern right now," Kingston counters.

"I don't give a shit what our greatest concern is. He was obsessed with her, King. You have no idea the shit he put her through."

"I can imagine," I interject. "And if anyone has a beef with the bastard, it's me. We'll take care of him too, I promise. But first, we need answers."

Kingston grits his teeth before finishing, "And we need them now."

TO BE CONTINUED….
Order Bitter Queen, Diece & Q's story Now

Interested in reading more by Kelsie Rae?
Signature Sweethearts Series

(Contemporary Romance Stand alones)

Liv

Luke

Breezy

Jude

Rhett

Sophie

Marcus

Anthony

Skye

Saylor

Advantage Play Series

(Romantic Suspense/Mafia Series)

Wild Card

Dark King

Little Bird

Bitter Queen

Stand Alones

Fifty-Fifty

Hired Hottie- Cocky Hero World

Drowning in Love

Bartered Souls Duet

(Urban Fantasy Series)

Gambled Soul

Wager Won

Sign up for Kelsie's newsletter to receive exclusive content, including the first two chapters of every new book two weeks before its release date!

Dear Reader,

I want to thank you guys from the bottom of my heart for taking a chance on Little Bird, and for giving me the opportunity to share this story with you. I couldn't do this without you!

I would also be very grateful if you could take the time to leave a review. It's amazing how such a little thing like a review can be such a huge help to an author!

Thank you so much!!!

-Kelsie

ALSO BY KELSIE RAE

Signature Sweethearts Series

(Contemporary Romance Stand alones)

Liv

Luke

Breezy

Jude

Rhett

Sophie

Marcus

Anthony

Skye

Saylor

Advantage Play Series

(Romantic Suspense/Mafia Series)

Wild Card

Dark King

Little Bird

Bitter Queen

Stand Alones

Fifty-Fifty

Hired Hottie- Cocky Hero World

Drowning in Love

Bartered Souls Duet

(Urban Fantasy Series)

<u>Gambled Soul</u>

<u>Wager Won</u>

Sign up for Kelsie's <u>newsletter</u> to receive exclusive content, including the first two chapters of every new book two weeks before its release date!

ABOUT THE AUTHOR

Kelsie is a sucker for a love story with all the feels. When she's not chasing words for her next book, you will probably find her reading or, more likely, hanging out with her husband and playing with her three kiddos who love to drive her crazy.

She adores photography, baking, her yorkie, her boxer, and her devon rex. Now that she's actively pursuing her writing dreams, she's set her sights on someday finding the self-discipline to not binge-watch an entire series on Netflix in one sitting.

If you'd like to connect with Kelsie, follow her on Facebook, sign up for her newsletter, or join Kelsie Rae's Reader Group to stay up to date on new releases, exclusive content, giveaways, and her crazy publishing journey.

Made in the USA
Columbia, SC
19 April 2025